JAMES WILLARD SCHULTZ

APIKUNI

Bear Chief's War Shirt

Edited by Wilbur Ward Betts

Illustrations by Glen Eagle Speaker

A Rendezvous Book

MOUNTAIN PRESS PUBLISHING CO.

Missoula, 1984

Library of Congress Cataloging in Publication Data

Schultz, James Willard 1859-1947.
  Bear Chief's war shirt.

  Summary: The author's novel of a Blackfeet Indian
chief whose sacred vision war shirt is stolen was
completed and published posthumously.
  1. Bear Chief (Siksika Indian)—Fiction. 2. Siksika
Indians—Fiction. (1. Siksika Indians—Fiction.
2. Indians of North America—Fiction) I. Betts, Wilbur
Ward. II. Eagle Speaker, Glen, ill. III. Title.
PS3537.C71176B4 1983   813'.52 (Fic)   83-23693
ISBN 0-87842-129-7
ISBN 0-87842-130-0 (pbk.)

Dedicated to the memory of my Blackfeet father Bird Rattler who adopted me at the Blood Sun Dance at Standoff, Alberta, Canada on July 13, 1936.

Wilbur Ward Betts

BIRD RATTLER *(Sis-cha-wan)*
by Glen Eagle Speaker

CONTENTS

Acknowledgments

An expression of gratitude is due the following persons for their assistance in the preparation of this book: my wife Roberta Van De Walker Betts; Mrs. Jessica Schultz Graham (Apaki), the late widow of James Willard Schultz; Montana State University Special Collections Librarian Minnie Paugh; Mrs. Diederika Seele, widow of the late Dr. Keith C. Seele; Eugene Lee Silliman, a Schultz scholar and editor; Richard Conn, Curator, Native Arts Department of the Denver Museum; and to Glen Eagle Speaker who acted as my consultant.

Introduction

This book involves a culture not familiar to most Americans. It recounts the way of life in a Blackfeet Indian Society, related by one of its members and describing a Piskan buffalo hunt, the capture of wild horses to be trained for the buffalo hunt, a typical Indian fight, the theft of horses, the scaffold burial of the dead, and day by day Indian living — food, clothing, shelter, and travel. Blackfeet Indian religious beliefs provide the book's central focus — the Sun God and the Above Ones, the sweat bath, and the Sun Dance with its Torture Dance and secret helpers. Bear Chief's War Shirt, which was real and does exist, is itself a religious symbol.

It is estimated that those belonging to the Blackfeet Tribes in the early 1800s numbered about 50,000. They were rulers of all the land from the Saskatchewan to the Yellowstone. Although the smallpox epidemic of the 1830s reduced their numbers about in half, they still remained powerful.

Nearly all historians, including Lewis and Clark, Prince Alexander Weid, George Catlin, Alexander Henry and John C. Ewers, emphasize the Blackfeet as a power to be reckoned with. Other Indian tribes as well as trappers and traders respected them. This power, coupled with their geographical location north of the usual routes of travel by white men, helped them retain their nomadic way of life, centuries old, almost without outside influence up to 1878, thus making this story possible.

"The author of this book," writes Harry C. James, "James Willard Schultz (Apikuni-Far-Away Whiterobe), was born August 26, 1859 at Boonville, New York. His parents were well cultured, well-to-do people. He was sent to Peekskill Military Academy in preparation for his entrance to West Point. In 1877 he went to St. Louis, Missouri to visit an uncle, Benjamin Stickney, who managed the Planters Hotel there. Intrigued by tales of trappers from Montana, he persuaded his mother to let him have five hundred dollars for a trip up the Missouri River. She advanced this sum to him exacting a promise that he would return home in the fall to complete his education." (He did not return until 1880 and stayed but a short time.) "On the Missouri River he met Joseph Kipp at Fort Benton. It was not long before they formed a partnership and set up a trading post at Carroll, the junction of the Musselshell and Missouri rivers. They were amazingly successful. In 1880 they took in four thousand one hundred buffalo robes for three dollars apiece and these they sold in Boston for seven dollars for each one."[*]

It was old Chief Running Crane who gave Schultz the name Ap-Pe-Kun-Ny (Spotted Robe), adopted him as his son, and took him into his tepee. With such close associations, Schultz in the first year had mastered the Indians' difficult language and also their sign language. He went on war parties and buffalo hunts with them. In 1879 he

---

[*] *The Piegan Storyteller*, Vol. 1 and 2; *The Piegan Storyteller Apikuni, As I Knew Him* by Harry C. James, Jan., April, 1976.

married one of their women, Piegan Natahki or Fine Shield Woman.

The near extermination of the buffalo, about 1883, brought an end to the nomadic life of the Blackfeet Indians. Schultz did some ranching, but he preferred to spend his time as a guide in the Rocky Mountains and in writing. During the balance of his life he wrote and had published thirty-seven books, true stories about Blackfeet Indians. Four additional books have been released and published posthumously since his death in 1947. Several other Schultz books are now being edited and will be published sometime in the future.

Lack of recognition during one's lifetime is often an accepted fact, as it was with James Willard Schultz. However, since his death in 1947, several factors have resulted in an increase in his popularity:

1. In the past few years there has been renewed interest in minorities, coming mainly from efforts of these groups to bring national attention to wrongs perpetrated on them by the white man. Many of Schultz' books touch on these injustices.

2. In 1975, David C. Andrews, of Andes, New York, formed the James Willard Schultz Society, with the help of Schultz' widow, Dr. Jessica Schultz Graham. The Society embraces over 200 members in the United States and Canada, including many of his old friends and associates, this editor among them.

3. On October 2, 1976, the birthplace of James Willard Schultz, at 153 Schuyler Street, Boonville, New York, was dedicated as a New York State Historical Landmark. Schultz' friends in the Society, including

ix

Joseph Conway, chairman of the Committee, made this dedication possible.

4. 1976, the year of the bicentennial, flushed from relative obscurity many historians and authors who otherwise might have been lightly passed over or completely forgotten, perhaps J. W. Schultz among them.

Wilbur W. Betts

Illustrations

THE ARTIST

Glen Eagle Speaker is a gifted artist rather than one who has been formally trained. He was educated at St. Paul's Residential Indian School on the Blood Indian Reservation at Standoff, Alberta, Canada. He teaches Indian heritage and conducts four Sacred Sweat Baths each year.

BEAR CHIEF AND THE SHADOWY OLD MAN

"Close by stood an Old Man wearing a strange war shirt – I saw that many small holes had been cut in the shirt."

Chapter 1
Bear Chief's Vision

In September 1901, Mr. Henry L. Stimson, Secretary of War, and his friend William H. Seward III climbed to the top of Chief Mountain, and there, where a buffalo could not possibly have climbed, they found an ancient and weather-worn buffalo skull. Where had it come from?

Chief Mountain. In the long-ago the Blackfeet Indians named it *Nina Istuki*, Chief Mountain, and the early adventurers of the Hudson's Bay Company took the name from the Blackfeet. 10,460 feet high, it stands at the northeastern edge of the present Glacier National Park, Montana. Its northern, eastern, and southern sides are great cliffs; its western, pine-clad side slopes steeply up to about three hundred yards from the mountain's flat summit, and from there on the ascent is a difficult one even for the most experienced mountain climber.

I am without doubt the only living white man who knows why that buffalo skull had been placed on top of Chief Mountain, and now, in my eighty-fourth year, I shall write the whole story, a story of interesting Indian religious belief and great adventure.

In June 1877, my mother gave me permission to go to

1

the Montana Territory for a buffalo hunt, I promising to return in time for the autumn term of Peekskill Military Academy, where I was a student. (I did not return until the autumn of 1880, and three weeks afterward was on my way back to the Montana plains: civilized life appalled me!)

On June 10th, 1877, in St. Louis, I boarded the Missouri River steamboat *Far West*, and in due time arrived in Fort Benton, Montana. There I met the noted Indian trader Joseph Kipp, whose father, Captain James Kipp, had been a prominent member of the powerful American Fur Company, and whose mother, Sakwi Ahki, was a member of the Mandan Indian Tribe and who became a second mother to me. Kipp and I at once had great liking for each other. I went with him to his trading post, Fort Conrad, on Marias River, eighty miles northwest of Fort Benton; and so I began a close association, which was to last until his death in 1913.

Soon after I arrived at Fort Conrad, the powerful Pikuni Tribe of the Blackfeet Indian Confederacy came to camp on the bottom land of the Marias, and Kipp introduced me to the chiefs, the medicine men, and other prominent members of the tribe. I went with them on big game hunts, beginning at once to learn their language and also sign language, wonderfully expressive and common to all the nomadic Plains Indian tribes, from the Saskatchewan River in Canada south to Mexico. Within a year I had mastered both languages.

As though it were yesterday, I vividly remember that June day of 1878 when Bear Chief's sacred, powerfully protecting war shirt was stolen; and equally well I remember our long and bloody quest to regain it. We were three hundred lodges of the Pikuni Tribe of the Blackfeet Indian Confederacy, camped on the small prairie at the

2

foot of Lower Two Medicine Lodges Lake, now Lower Two Medicine Lake, Glacier National Park. I say we, for I was, and still am, a member of the tribe, having been adopted by one of its chiefs, brave old Running Crane. At that time, I was living with Bear Chief, tall, well proportioned, handsome, long haired, and of about thirty winters. His two wives were sisters, both of them of medium height and slender, with pleasant features and hair braids so long the ends fell well below their knees. The elder one, Fox Woman, Bear Chief's "Sits-Beside-Him Woman," shared his couch at the back of the lodge. Badger Woman's couch was at the south side, mine at the north side of the lodge. The doorways of Blackfeet lodges always faced the east.

Tied to the lodge poles behind Bear Chief's couch were his sacred powerfully protecting shield, war bonnet, and war shirt, the shield in buckskin cover and bonnet and shirt painted and fringed parfleche cylinders about ten inches in diameter and two feet in length.

That morning, just before sunrise, Fox Woman was first to awaken. *"Ki kistapi tupiks, nipwoat,"* ("You nothing ones, arise"), she called, taking down her man's shield, cased war bonnet, and war shirt, carrying them out to hang upon a tripod of red-painted pine sticks close to the back of the lodge. This was always the procedure on stormless days, so that Sun could continue infusing them with his sacred, strength-giving light. Bear Chief and I, each in a blanket wrap, hurried to join the hundreds of men and boys bathing in the lake. Winter and summer alike, bathing every morning was the unavoidable duty of all Blackfeet males from three years to old age. In summer, the women and girls bathed later in the day; in winter, they took to the sweat lodges they had built.

The sun was just up when Bear Chief and I returned to

3

the lodge and dressed under cover of our blankets, then combing our hair. The women were broiling deer ribs and steeping a kettle of Kutenai tea for us, but we were not to eat there. As always, many men standing just outside their doorways were shouting invitations to certain friends to eat and smoke. We heard old Red Eagle, powerful medicine man, owner of the ancient and sacred Thunder Bird pipe, and familiar with its hours-long ritual of prayers, songs, and dances, shouting our names along with those of other friends. His was a large lodge made of twenty buffalo cow hides tanned into soft white leather cut to shape and sinew-sewed together. On its north and south sides were painted large, black birds representing his sacred pipe. On the back of the lodge, close to its top, was a red and black painting resembling a Maltese cross; it was the symbol of the butterfly, giver of good visions, or as the whites say, dreams.

When we entered the lodge, Red Eagle gave us an *Okyi* of greeting, motioned us to sit on the couch of one of his four wives, at the north side of the lodge. The women were gathered on the south side, preparing us the feast. Other guests were Ancient Man, White Antelope, and Little Plume, of our tribe; White Beaver, a Flathead; and Bear Hat, a Kutenai. About a month earlier, a dozen families of each tribe had come from West-side-of-the-Rockies to camp with us and hunt, and were enjoying our hospitality.

We were soon eating the feast the women had cooked: broiled bighorn ribs, boiled wild turnips, good strong soup. That finished, Red Eagle filled a large stone pipe — not his sacred one — with a fragrant mixture of tobacco and one herb we loved, and by turns we smoked it. On the previous afternoon, the Crazy Dogs band of warriors, of which Bear Chief and I were members, had given its

4

spectacular dance, and now, after several of our visitors had told of their interest in it, one of them, White Beaver, the Flathead, said to Bear Chief in sign language: "My friend, the war shirt you wore in the dance is beautiful. The red-quilled sun on its bosom, the blue-quilled morning star on its back, its sleeve fringes of ermine skins, they are especially beautiful. Yet it has one great fault: the many small holes you have cut in it — were you to wear it in winter weather, you would freeze."

To that Bear Chief, both orally and with signs, replied: "My friend, my war shirt is just as my powerful vision helper told me to make it. He strongly said that I must make the many holes in it, for they would prevent enemy bullets or enemy arrows or enemy knives doing so. Well, my friend, I have worn that shirt in seven fights with our enemies, and not once have I been even slightly wounded."

At that, White Beaver and Bear Hat clapped hand to mouth, expressive of surprise, and both signed to him: "Your vision. Tell us of it."

Bear Chief, looking askance at Red Eagle, said to him: "Sun's Man, sacred one, perhaps this is not the time nor the place for me to do as they ask."

"Oh, tell it, fully tell it! Never will I tire of hearing you tell of your vision," Red Eagle replied, and others voiced their interest in it. And Red Eagle added: "Begin the telling of it. At once! I will keep on refilling the pipe as needed."

I had not seen many winters when I began asking my father to permit me to endure my sacred fast, Bear Chief began. But always he would reply that I was not old enough or experienced enough to rightly pray to Sun to give me a powerful vision, a vision that would reveal to me someone who would become my sacred protector, and so enable me to live to very old age. Came my twentieth winter; then summer, and from Bear River (Marias) we moved northward and made camp on the prairie at the lower end of First Inside Lake (St. Mary). There, day after day, I looked at Chief Mountain, not far to the north of us, and thought that its summit would be a good place for me to endure my fast. In our lodge one evening I spoke of it, and my mother cried: 'Oh, no! Not away up there, so far from us. Have your sacred fast somewhere near, so that we can daily see that you are safe in your time of hunger and prayer.'

But said my father: 'You are right, my son. Way up there, far from our camp, no one will appear to break your fast, your vision-seeking sleep. Tomorrow we will have Spotted Bear pray for you, paint you, and on the next day I will go up there with you!'

'Oh, no! Not up there! So high! So far from us! Oh husband, have pity for our son, for me,' my mother cried.

'Woman, absolutely cease your talk of this,' my father replied. 'I want our son to go there because it is very high; so he will be that much nearer Sun and all of the Above People, to whom he must pray for help in his quest of a powerful vision.'

Well, the next afternoon Spotted Bear, possessor of the sacred Elk Tongue pipe and bundle, painted a red sun on my forehead and, helped by some of his sacred friends, gave his long ritual of prayers, songs, and dances for me. It was all so powerfully affecting that when he had me take the pipe and dance with it, I wept.

On the following morning, my father and I saddled our horses and started for the mountain, I taking along two buffalo robes for my couch. We had not gone far from camp when we came to a small bare ridge and my father, bringing us to a stop at its crest, pointed to a whitened buffalo bull skull, saying: 'Son, as you know, you were born right where we are now camped. On the day of your birth, I came up this way to hunt, saw the lone bull grazing there, and, leaving my horse, crept close and killed the buffalo. That morning your mother said she was hungry for liver. Well, before mid-day she ate two slices of the bull's liver that my father broiled for her. Said your mother when she finished: 'My man, Sun favors us; he has done much for us this day. I wanted a son. I have him. I wanted liver, and you soon brought me plenty of it.'

'My son,' said my father, 'I feel sure that this is a good luck skull. I am going to take it along for your pillow. I advise that you pray to it also.'

With that, he took up the skull, and we rode on, were soon in the pines that cover the steeply rising west side of the great mountain. Soon the slope became so steep that we had often to let our horses stop to regain their breath, but we did ride them to the upper edge of the pines and there tied them and went on — up the steep rise of rock, often pausing to rest and get our breath. So at last we came to the very top, long, but not wide, and at one point flat. There I put down my buffalo robes, and my father laid the buffalo skull beside them; there on that high level place I would endure my fast. We stood for awhile, silent, looking off from that great height. Far to the east, plainly in sight, were our Kutoyists, the Sweetgrass Hills. To the southeast, still farther away, we could see, though dimly, the tops of our Ispitsists, the Highwood Mountains. I loved our mountains near and far, our almost endless buffalo plains, and I loved most of all this high Chief Mountain, upon whose top we stood.

A long time my father and I looked off across our plains and mountains, and at last he said: 'My son, I must go, leaving you to your lone fast, your vision-seeking. Pray almost constantly. Pray especially to Sun, Moon, Morning Star, the Seven Men (the Pleiades), and the Great Dipper to powerfully help you. Tomorrow, and at mid-day every day thereafter, I will come with our horses to where they are now tied and wait until near sunset for you to come down and ride home with me; that is, when you have had your vision. For if you are long about it, you will be hungry and weak, unable to walk home. Take courage and do not forget that your mother and I, Red Eagle, Spotted Bear, and others of your friends will be praying that you may soon have a powerful vision.' And with that, he left me.

I smoothed out my buffalo robes, lay down upon them pillowing my head upon the buffalo skull, and prayed to the Above People to pity me, to give me a powerful vision. I lay there a long time praying, praying, but I could not sleep. I left my couch, sat at the rim of the cliff of the great mountain and looked down upon our plains. I could see, near and far, herds of buffalo, some grazing and resting, others strung out in narrow formation as they traveled to and from their water holes. Not far away a herd was running out from Rope-Stretched-Across Creek (Lee's Creek). Some hunters of our brother tribe the Bloods were running them with their fast buffalo horses, making a good killing, I thought. Then came an eagle with a rabbit hanging from its claws. It lighted not far from me, began tearing the rabbit apart with its sharp bill and eating of it. This made me feel hungry. Sun loves eagles, giving them strength to go up nearer him than any other bird. 'Oh you high flying one, you always-successful taker of the food you want, help me to soon have a vision, a helpful vision,' I prayed. Finished eating, the eagle flew up, circled above me four times and then went westward, and I thought, 'It has circled four times, four the sacred number. Ha! Maybe that is his way of saying he will give me help.'

I sat there at the edge of the great cliff until Sun went to his far-off island home; then I turned back to my buffalo robes, getting between them, my head on the buffalo skull. Long, long I prayed Sun and all of the Above People to help me, to give me a powerful vision, but the Seven-Person-Men, ever turning, gave me to know that it was past midnight when at last I slept. I slept until rising Sun awakened me, but I had no vision. I was desperate for food

8

and water. Seekers of sacred visions may not have food, but they may have water. At the top of the north side of the mountain, I had seen a thick long stretch of ice. I went to it, chipped off some small pieces with my knife, letting them one by one melt slowly in my mouth; and so I lost my thirst — now strong enough to keep on praying for a sacred vision. All day long I sat at the edge of the great cliff, praying often to the Above People and to all the birds and animals that I could see. In the small pines at the foot of the cliff were many elk and deer rubbing against one another, against the trees and brush, unable to lie down and sleep because of the swarms of flies. I pitied them, asked that they pity me, help me to obtain a sacred vision.

As Sun was going down behind the Backbone (Rocky Mountains), I went to the ice bank, ate more of it, and then lay down on my couch, praying longer than ever to the Above Ones to pity me, to help me obtain a sacred vision. Soon I slept. Sun, shining in my eyes, awakened me, and I felt sad: I had not been given a vision of any kind. Was it that in the past I had offended the Above Ones? I remembered that when I was of but few winters, I had one day come upon an otter hide tied to a branch of a tree. My father had the hides of three otter he had trapped. He and my mother often talked about the supplies they would get for them at a trader's house: sugar, tea, flour, cartridges, blankets. As for myself, I wanted sugar, plenty of sugar, and with this otter hide my mother would get plenty of it for me, for me alone. I pulled the hide from the branch, soon ran into our lodge with it, crying: 'Mother, see! This my otter hide; you will get me plenty of sugar for it.'

'You, boy, where did you get it?' my father shouted.

'Out there in the timber. It was tied to a tree.'

At once my mother began crying, and my father powerfully scolded: 'Oh, you bad, you worthless boy! You have stolen someone's sacrifice to Sun! So is it that you have made Him angry at you, at your mother and me for having you. In one way or another, He will make us suffer for this what you have done to Him.'

With that, he seized my arm and yanked me out of the lodge, and there we stood, he shouting again and again that I had stolen someone's otter hide sacrificed to Sun and that whoever had given the hide should come and get it. The people hurried from their lodges to listen, stare at us, and I heard the nearer ones saying what a terrible sin I had committed — my theft of the sacred sacrifice might make Sun angry at our whole tribe.

Limping and wailing came old Red Crow, saying that it was his Sun offering that I had stolen. My father gave him the otter skin. He was glad to get it and hurried to tie it again to the branch of the tree, we going with him. There he prayed Sun to forgive my theft. My father had brought along a large stone pipe, my mother a pair of beautifully quilled moccasins she had made for me. They tied them to other branches of the tree, praying Sun to accept them; to forgive me the wrong I had done Him; to pity me, help me in every way; and to give us all long and full life.

Well, Sun seemed to have been pleased with their sacrifices, to have granted their prayers; for winter after winter, summer after summer, we prospered in every way. But now, when for the first time I was praying to Him for his powerful aid, for a helpful vision, I did not receive it. Was that because of my long-ago theft of His sacred otter hide? Lying there under my buffalo robe, my head on the buffalo skull, I trembled, felt weak. But I prayed on and on until my mouth burned, dried, and I could no longer speak. At last I slept, but was given no vision. Oh, my sadness was terrible.

Praying, sleeping upon my robe couch, sitting out at the edge of the cliff, and occasionally going for more ice, I became weaker and more sad. At last it was my fourth night there on the top of Chief Mountain. Four, the sacred good luck number for us and our brother tribes. But would it bring good luck for me? I had no hope of it. Although now I could only whisper, whispering I prayed to Sun, Morning

10

Star, and all the other sacred ones up there in the blue. I prayed often also to my pillow, as my father had advised. Also, I often looked off at the Seven Men, moving, always moving, in that way giving us of the earth the way to keep track of the passing of night. At last I saw that they were in their middle-night position, and then I slept. The white light of coming day was in the eastern sky when I awoke, and I was happy! Exultant! Sun and his Above Ones had pitied me, given me a vision.

In my vision, I walked in the timbered valley of a river, Bear River (Marias) it seemed to be; I asked all the animals I saw for help. But one and all they turned from me, went their various ways. Then, discouraged, I returned to my couch, and far below me on a sand shore of the river was sitting a water animal, and lo, he did not turn and swim away when I called to him for help.

'Young man,' he said, 'I do pity you. I will help you. That war shirt, look at it carefully, very carefully.' Ha! As he said that, there close by stood an old man wearing a strange war shirt. The old one turned his back to me, again faced me, and I saw that many small holes had been cut in the shirt. And that certain water animal said to me: 'Young man, you will make a shirt like that. You will fringe it with ermine skins; your mother will quill the red sun symbol on its bosom, the blue Morning Star symbol on its back, and then you will cut many holes in it. Young man, those holes are of great power; they will prevent your enemies from making holes in it and so killing you. Also, if you take good care of it, the shirt will help you in all your undertakings so that you will live to very old age.' Having said that, he and the shadowy old man in the war shirt vanished. I got up then. Sun was rising. I gave Him my buffalo head pillow, my two robes, and using my gun as a cane staggered down to the edge of the pines. Soon my father came riding up bringing a horse for me. At once I told him of my vision, and he said that it was powerful; that water animals seemed to be more Sun-favored than

11

those of the land.

Thus Bear Chief completed the remarkable story of his vision. Although they remained impassive throughout, Red Eagle, who had refilled the pipe as needed, Bear Hat, and the others had listened with intense interest — for them the vision had expressed the realilty and closeness of the Above Ones. At the end of the story, the listeners signed their approval and appreciation: "Sun is good to you, Bear Chief. Long will you live." (No member of the Blackfeet tribes ever gave the specific name of the animal of a vision lest the vision lose its beneficent power. Thus Bear Chief's "certain water animal" might have been a beaver or an otter, a mink or a muskrat.)

It was the height of the season of countless swarms of biting, stinging flies that infested the mountain country. The elk, deer, and moose had moved high up, even to the bare rocky slopes above the pines, to escape them. The several thousand horses of our camp were so crazed by them that from dawn to dark, unable to graze or rest, they rubbed against one another, occasionally breaking into long swift, and useless, runs. We had come up to the lake for the purpose of obtaining new lodge poles, and now that the women had cut, peeled, and dried all that were needed, our chiefs, after counciling together, sent out their camp crier to announce that, on the following day, because of our suffering horses, we would break camp and head for some place well out on the plains, where flies were few. Later, Bear Chief came from the council and told his women and me that, as the people still had many winter buffalo robes and furs they wanted to trade for white men's goods, we were to head for Many Houses (Fort Benton) and camp on Mile River (Teton), just over the ridge to the north of it. That was cheerful news for the women — they had great need of new blankets, dress goods, sugar, beads, and other necessities, and now they would soon be trading for them. They sang happily as they went on with their work, gathering wood for the lodge fire and preparing our evening meal.

"Kyi! Kakitsoyit! — There! You eat!" said Fox Woman, as she set plates of broiled deer meat before Bear Chief and me. And then, "Sun sets: I go to bring in your sacred things."

Singing and lightly dancing, she left us, went on singing, and then suddenly yelled, "Bear Chief! Oh, my man! Your sacred war shirt! Gone, stolen, your sacred vision war shirt!"

"Oh, no! No! It can't be stolen!" cried Bear Chief, and he sprang up, ran out of the lodge, Badger Woman and I closely following. Already a crowd of men and women were gathering around wailing Fox Woman, who was standing beside the tripod close back of the lodge. We pushed our way to her and could hardly believe our eyes when we saw that the parfleche cylinder containing the war shirt was missing. Bear Chief stood frowning, silently staring at the tripod and the shield and war bonnet placed upon it. He seemed not to hear this one and that one uselessly asking how the war shirt could have been stolen during the day, when it was constantly within sight of our people moving about the camp. For only a moment the distraught man stood there, then he slowly went back into the lodge, Fox Woman at his heels with the war bonnet shield, and then Badger Woman and I. He sat down on his couch, bent over, the most forlorn man that I had ever seen. Fox Woman tied the shield and war bonnet at their proper places above his couch, then sat down beside him, drew him to her, and sadly and repeatedly wailed: "Gone it is, my man's vision-giving war shirt!

13

Stolen, my man's sacred war shirt. Oh Sun! Be not angry at him; it is not his fault that it is gone. Blame me; make me suffer because I did not more closely watch it, especially now, when some of the Other-Side-Of-The-Mountains People are camped with us."

Chapter 2

Piskan Buffalo Hunt

Fox Woman continued wailing pitiful pleas to Sun to blame her for the loss of the war shirt, Bear Chief remaining supinely in her arms. Silent and grim faced Badger Woman sat motionless upon her couch. One after another our head chiefs came in — White Calf, our head chief; the lesser chiefs Running Crane, Three Stars, Little Plume, Tail-Feathers-Coming-Over-The-Hill; and war chief Little Dog. As Bear Chief did not look at nor speak to them, it devolved upon me to be the host. I welcomed them, motioned them to seats upon the couches, filled my big stone pipe with the right mixture of tobacco and kaksin, and passed it to White Calf. He lit the pipe with a coal from the fire, blew a few whiffs of smoke to the Above Ones and to Earth Mother, then passed the pipe to the next guest on his right, saying: "Fox Woman, at once cease your wailing. Bear Chief, my friend, take courage. Let us try to find some way to recover your sacred war shirt."

Fox Woman instantly obeyed his order. Bear Chief shrugged his shoulders, sat up, and said, "Who could have dared to steal it?"

"One of these Kutenai or Flathead men camping with us took it! Walking slowly and easily, seeing that no one's eyes were upon him, he snatched the war shirt from the tripod, put it under his wrap and went on," cried Fox Woman.

Said Running Crane: "I am sure that the woman is mistaken. None of our West-side friends camping with us would have dared to take it; they know as well as we do that Sun terribly punishes the thief who takes sacred-vision relics."

"Right you are," said Little Plume. "They do not forget that in the long ago a Kutenai man named Big Otter stole the shield of our chief, Low Horns, and that, a few nights later, the thief died on his couch, the shield tightly clasped to his breast."

Said White Calf: "Unless crazy, no one of our visiting friends nor of us would have taken the war shirt. And neither is crazy, I am sure that one of our many enemies, unaware of the Sun-power of the war shirt made off with it."

"If that is so, just think how crazy-brave he is, that enemy thief," I put in.

Said Tail-Feathers-Coming-Over-The-Hill: "We know nothing about our various enemy tribes except that we fight them, kill many of them. It may be that this war shirt thief can in some way safely keep it."

"There is but one action for us: Pray Sun to give a vision that will enable us to recover the sacred war shirt," Little Dog forcefully exclaimed, and to this suggestion every one of our little circle gave quick assent, Bear Chief himself suddenly straightening up and exclaiming: "Yes, that we must do. Ha! I now have strong feeling right here within me, that Sun will heed our prayers."

Bear Chief then took over the refilling of the pipe, and

16

the talk turned to our breaking camp the next morning and the route we would take. At last the fourth pipeful was smoked, and Bear Chief, ostentatiously knocking out the ashes, exclaimed, "There! It is burned out!" as he dismissed our guests.

Every man of our camp had that evening, as on every evening, brought in his fast buffalo horses and tied them close to his lodge, where they would have some protection from night-prowling enemies. In the morning none of them were missing; but when we came to rounding up our herds out on the prairie, we soon found that enemies had been among them in the night: from Raven Child's band ten had been stolen, Little Otter had lost eleven, and fifteen were gone from Lone Man's largest band of all, more than two hundred head.

"Let us all scatter out, try to find where these enemies camped, for there we may find some of their belongings that will let us know who they are," said Little Dog, but look though we did, near and far, our search was fruitless; we did not even learn in what direction they had gone with our horses.

So was it that we did not break camp until the following morning. Sadly our Kutenai and Flathead friends helped us prepare to leave. They would not go with us, and they dared not remain there without our protection. They would, they said, move back into their West-side country on the following day. It was all of ten o'clock when, a mile or more below the lake, we left the river valley and strung out across the green prairie, headed southeast. And what a grand and thrilling sight it was, that more than a mile long traveling procession of our Pikuni Tribe. Far in the lead, as scouts, rode members of the various bands of our Ikuni Katsiks (All Friends, as this warrior society was named). Then came our chiefs with some of our Sun

17

priests, so-called medicine men; and then family after family on their gaily decorated riding horses, their travois horses, and their horses drawing the long poles of the lodges. In the rear of each family came their loose horses, anywhere from fifty to two hundred, some with packs and herded along by the youngsters. In all, the tribe owned about five thousand horses. Some of the children rode in the comfortable buffalo robe-lined travois, others on gentle horses of their own. Trotting along after each family were its many dogs, one kind huge, savage, wolf-like; the other of coyote size and shape. Strangely enough, the two kinds never interbred. To be safe from attack from the wolf-like dogs, white men in our camp were obliged to go about wearing blankets or buffalo robes, in the Indian way.

Chatting, laughing, and at times a dozen or more of the families breaking out with cheerful song, our long procession rode on and on. Occasional herds of antelope fled from our approach, but our hunters did not pursue them; we were not after meat that day. Near sunset we turned down into the valley of Two Medicine Lodges River and made camp right where, in the long-ago, the stream had received its name. At the upper end of a long wide stretch of valley prairie and close to a cottonwood grove, the Pikuni that summer had planned to put up their annual sacrifice to Sun, the Okan, His Vision, or as our early Indian traders inappropriately named it, Medicine Lodge. Then soon came a brother tribe, the Kainah Many Chiefs, now Blood Tribe of Alberta, who also built their Sun offering, so there and then the stream was named *Natoki Okan Isisakta* — Two-His-Vision River. The Holy Family Mission of the Jesuits now stands where we camped that night.

After Bear Chief and I had helped his women unpack

18

and unsaddle the many horses that had carried and drawn their lodge skin, lodge poles, and the many parfleches and bundles of food, clothing, pots and pans, blankets, buffalo robes and furs, we sat with a circle of our friends while the women were putting up the lodge, gathering firewood, and preparing a meal for us. Close north of our camp, a long high cliff forms the rim of the valley, and at one place at its foot, an acre or more in extent, are layer after layer of buffalo bones, buffalo horn tips, and wads of buffalo fur to a depth of five or six feet. For there, in the long-ago, had been one of the many *piskans* of the Blackfeet tribes. The Blackfeet had had these *piskans* here and there on every stream of their once vast territory, from the Saskatchewan River south to the Yellowstone River.

Translated literally, the word *piskan* means "corral." But to the Blackfeet it meant much more — it was the name for their deadly contrivance by which they slaughtered a whole herd of buffalo at one time. At the foot of a cliff they built a huge corral of dead and fallen trees, of tree branches and brush, the cliff its rear side. At the top of the cliff, directly above the corral, they set up piles of stones in two ever-diverging lines, like a great letter V, for about a mile. In each of the Blackfeet tribes were always three or four men termed *ahwa wiwakiks*, buffalo callers. They were men of great bravery, ever sacrificing their best to Sun, to have His help in their dangerous work. Whenever the Blackfeet decided they needed a great quantity of meat and hides, they watched for a buffalo herd to come grazing just beyond a little ridge of the plain, near the outer ends of the V-shaped lines of rock piles. When at last a herd of buffalo was seen to be in the right position, hundreds of men and women hurried out and lay down flat at the rock pile to which each had been

19

assigned; then, before the advent of horses in the North-west in about 1700, a buffalo caller ran to the little ridge just beyond the rock lines. Cautiously he neared its top; if the herd was still in the right position, a little way out from him, he wrapped his buffalo robe, fur side out, close to his body and, bent over, went down the ridge a little way, hopped about flapping his wrap and crying "Hoo hoo! Hoo hoo!" The buffalo had never seen a creature like this; they ceased grazing, stared at the "caller." Still hopping and hoo hooing, he turned back up the ridge, moving over its crest and out of sight of the herd. But not for long; he was soon back on the crest, continuing his antics and cries, retreating and reappearing until the buffalo had to find out what this strange creature was. Young cows were the most inquisitive, at first walking and then running toward the ridge; soon the whole herd was following them. The caller meanwhile was running down the inner side of the ridge, heading for the open end of the V, where the *awpwotaks* — frighteners, were gathered. He soon entered the V, heading for the cliff, the buffalo gaining on him. Then, when the buffalo were well in between the lines, the frighteners began rising up on each side of them, shouting and waving their wraps. No longer did they follow the decoyer — he had disappeared, joining one of the groups at the rock piles. The buffalo had to keep running straight ahead, their only way of escaping from the constantly rising and shouting people. When the leaders of the herd came to the cliff, they could not stop nor turn aside, owing to pressure from behind, off it they plunged, the others blindly following, into the corral below.

As we sat there at that near-sundown time, Bear Chief again bent over, forlorn of face, mourning the loss of his war shirt, we tried to cheer him. Old Big Swan pointed to

20

the cliff and said: "Bear Chief, friend, listen: I was about five or six winters when I first saw our people stage a successful *piskan*. We had been camping here for some time, our scouts daily up there on top watching for a buffalo herd to come near enough to be decoyed. Daily our sacred ones sacrificed their best to Sun, praying Him to soon help us in a successful slaughtering of buffalo. Like all the other frighteners, every evening my mother prayed: 'Oh Sun! Oh all of you Above Ones! Pity me, help me. Soon I go out to help frighten the buffalo. Oh, let them not swerve and trample us. Make them run straight to the cliff and off it!'

"One evening after she had prayed, I said to her: 'When you go out there to the stone piles, I shall go with you. I want to be a frightener.'

" 'Oh, no! No! You are too young for that. Frighteners are always in danger of being trampled. You can't go with me,' she answered.

" 'Boys must learn early to be brave; so is it that he shall go with you,' my father told me.

" 'He shall not go — he so small!' she yelled.

" 'Not too young; he absolutely goes with you,' he shouted back.

"My mother seized me, hugged me, saying: 'If he goes up there, you will take him, not I. Never again will I be one of the frighteners.'

" 'Again you have your way; you make of me a nothing man,' my father told her, and taking up his wrap, he left us. Himself one of the corral men, he could not take me up to join the frighteners.

"Not long after that, as we were eating our morning meal, our camp crier began shouting: 'You frighteners! You frighteners! Our scouts report a buffalo herd has come. Hurry up to your frightening places, for already the

21

PISKAN BUFFALO HUNT
by Glen Eagle Speaker

"A swift brown river of the buffalo began falling from the cliff down into the corral."

decoyer is on his way there.'

"Neither my mother nor my father spoke — she rushed to join the frighteners, but my father snatched up his rifle and seized my arm, forcing me to run to the corral with him. We climbed to the top and sat, as already many of the corral men were doing, the rest of them hurrying to it. My father talked with the nearest of the sitters, but I did not listen; I kept my eyes on the top of the cliff straight above us. Long we sat there waiting, waiting for what we hoped would happen. Said one, 'We have been here a long time — perhaps the herd has run away.'

"Said my father: 'Never has Old Bull failed to decoy a herd. Ha! Listen!'

"Faintly at first, then louder and still more loud, came to our ears the shouting of the frighteners, and then like a swift brown river, the buffalo began hurtling from the cliff down into the corral. The lead ones struck the ground with a thunderous sound, one of them bursting open, its blood and entrails redly rising, scattering like rain. Tumbling over and over, they came down headfirst, and every other way; in no time at all the whole herd piled up, a little mountain of dead, dying, and crippled buffalo; some of the last were unhurt and at once sought a way of escape, only to be quickly shot down by my father and the other corral men. That done, they gathered to sit and smoke while waiting for the frighteners to come down by a trail west of the cliff to take their part in butchering the dead herd. But first came the decoyer himself, riding a brown horse, on whose head was tied the skin of a buffalo head — horns, ears, whiskers, and all; and he in a buffalo robe, lying flat to imitate the hump — no wonder the buffalo thought him a strange one of their kind as they heard his hoo hooing and watched his appearing and disappearing at the top of the ridge. He had been successful in his work. Safe work, so different from that of our far-back decoyers, who, before the time of horses were sometimes trampled to death by an onrushing herd.

"As the decoyer came riding into the corral, men hurried to meet him as they shouted: 'Old Bull! Old Bull! Sun-powered is Old Bull! Food he has brought us! A real man is Old Bull!'

"Then my father, leader of the corral men, said to him: 'Old Bull, dismount, look over these of your decoying and choose one of them for your women and children.'

"Old Bull's choice was a fat, dry cow of three winters. Came then the frighteners, completing the whole tribe of us gathered at the corral enclosing the little mountain of dead buffalo, two hundred and seventy-three of them including the calves, as we afterward counted. We opened the corral in places and this and that family, both afoot and with horses, drew out allotted buffalo to where they could be easily butchered. Many, of course, were butchered within the corral. So was it that before night our camp was red with lines of drying meat. Ha! We were a happy people in those days."

"Hai-ya! Hai-ya!" Running Crane mournfully exclaimed. "But for Many-Tail-Feathers' vision we would still be using our *piskans!*" To that all gave sad assent, and the talk turned to a more pleasant subject.

I had heard the famous story of Many-Tail-Feathers many times, best told by Many-Tail-Feathers' son, my good friend now dead.

Nine miles above the town of Choteau, Montana, on the south side of the Teton River valley, is the bone-strewn site of the once favorite *Ahksi Omaipiskan* — Good *Piskan* (corral) of the Pikuni tribe of the Blackfeet Indian Confederacy. Close above it is a flat-topped butte upon which, in the very-long-ago, members of the tribe, with many large white stones set out the figure of a man, arms outstretched, to represent one of their gods, a most powerful god named *Napi*, Old Man. So was the butte named *Napi Aiakisa Pahwikwiyi*, Old-Man-Lying-Butte, and it was believed that Old Man himself, in some mysterious way was the cause of the constant success the tribe had with the *piskan*.

My friend Many-Tail-Feathers, Crow Eyes, the name of his youth, died in 1925, in his ninetieth year. In his eighth summer (summer of 1843), the Pikuni moved from Bear River (Marias River) over to Milk River (Teton River) and made camp at the foot of Old-Man-Lying-Butte, hoping soon to slaughter a buffalo herd in the nearby *piskan*, my friend's father, Many-Tail-Feathers, to be the decoyer. He had been a decoyer for many winters, had never once failed in his work, so the people had great faith in him. On the fourth morning of the encampment, scouts reported a buffalo herd in the right position for decoying, and led by Many-Tail-Feathers on his looks-like-a-buffalo horse, the frighteners hurried out to their places at the long lines of rock piles. Much sooner than usual the decoyer had the herd chasing him; he turned aside, and the frighteners drove the herd straight into the *piskan*. Then happily singing, praising the decoyer, saying again and again that it was a Sun-favored day for them, the people butchered the herd. Night came and, tired by their long hard work, all soon took to their couches and slept. Then, near morning, Crow Eyes' mother awakened him, held him close and wailed: "Oh, son! Your father is not here. I have been long awake, expecting him to soon appear. But he does not come. Oh, I fear that he is in trouble; dead, perhaps; killed by enemies somewhere out there."

"Let us go out and look for him," the boy proposed.

"Oh, no! No! Enemies are probably out there. Oh, what

25

shall we do — cry out, arouse the people?"

Then it was that an old man named Bear Paw began shouting: "Awake, you sleepers! Hurry! Come running! The *piskan* is burning!"

Men were shouting, frightened women and children were crying, as out from their lodges they came and saw that the *piskan* really was burning. Crow Eyes' mother cried: "Not here, my man! Long gone, my man! Enemies have killed him and are burning the *piskan!*"

Seizing their weapons, the men ran toward the *piskan* but soon met Many-Tail-Feathers, he shouting and signing to them to stop, to turn back; when they had come to a halt, he cried out so that all could hear: "My friends, return to your lodges. I set fire to the *piskan*; you can not save it. Be not angry at me: because of my vision I had to do it."

Some of the crowd angrily shouted that he had done them a great wrong; others asked that he tell of his vision, and he answered that he would do so later on.

Sun was well up when the chiefs and other wise ones of the tribe, after eating their morning meal, gathered in the decoyer's lodge to hear him tell of his vision; after they had smoked a pipe to the Above Ones and to Earth Mother, he said to them: "My friends, my vision was very powerful. It was that I was walking in a valley strange to me when a buffalo bull came from a grove, stopped, and raised his right forefoot as though making the sign for peace. 'Peace! Peace!' I signed. Then we met, and he said: 'I have been looking for you. You and your kind are doing us a great wrong. With your *piskans* you are rapidly killing off us buffalo. If you keep doing this, you will put an end to us. So this I say: Stop using your *piskans* if you would prevent a dread future for your tribe and all your kind.'

"What would it be, this dreadful happening?" he asked.

26

'I have warned you; I will say no more,' the bull answered, and turned away. With that, the man awoke. He was trembling, his body wet with sweat. He felt that he must at once prove to his vision-buffalo that he had accepted the warning, accepted it not only for himself but for all his people. So was it that he hurried to the *piskan* and set it afire.

Said Lone Walker, the head chief, when the decoyer had finished: "Many-Tail-Feathers, you did right to burn the *piskan*. What our Sun-given visions tell us to do, so must we do if we are to survive the dangers that beset us."

Right there and then the council decided that the Pikuni would never again use a *piskan* to obtain food. Then Many-Tail-Feathers, following the order of the council, visited the Bloods and the Blackfeet to tell them his vision, and they too heeded its warning. Thus all three tribes of the Blackfeet Indian Confederacy ended the use of *piskans*.

On our fourth evening out from Two Medicine Lodges River, we made camp on Teton River, just north of Fort Benton, and nearly every family argued long about what, on the morrow, they should buy with their buffalo robes and furs. My friend Bear Chief was not interested in this talk; crossly he said to his wives: "Trade for whatever you want. It matters not to me what you get." I wondered if he would ever cease mourning the loss of his war shirt.

There were five trading firms in Fort Benton: I. G. Baker and Company; T. C. Power and Brother; Murphy and Neal; Weatherwax and Wetzel; and Kleinsmidt. However, I. G. Baker and Company always received the bulk of Blackfeet trade because a member of the firm, kind generous Charles E. Conrad, or Spotted Fur Cap, as he was affectionately named, was married to a woman of the Blood Tribe. He spoke the Blackfeet language almost

27

perfectly and was even a member of the Kit Foxes, one of the warrior societies.

The next morning we all headed for I. G. Baker's big log store, all of us dressed in our best, men riding in the lead, women following with their pack horses and travois horses loaded with robes and furs. We topped the ridge and paused to look down on the little town. At its lower end stood the big, adobe fort, in which several companies of the Third Infantry were quartered. Above the fort, a row of stores and saloons faced the river; back of them were scattered the homes of the residents.

And lo! Five steamboats were tied at the levee, unloading goods they had brought up from St. Louis, 2,100 miles by river.

As we neared the store, Chief Running Crane shouted: "Now, my children, the All-Friends song." We sang it happily, and Spotted Fur Cap came to greet us as we dismounted before the store. Soon the chiefs and I were sitting with him in his office, smoking the big pipe that he had filled, talking with him about this and that. After a while, he said to Bear Chief: "My friend, is it true you have lost your war shirt?"

"Yes. It was stolen from me, right in daytime stolen," Bear Chief sadly answered.

"Ha! I knew that it was your war shirt — the many little holes cut in it, the patched place on its right sleeve. Oh, I knew that it was your war shirt."

Springing up from his seat quivering, Bear Chief cried: "Oh, Spotted Fur Cap! When did you see it? Who had it, my sacred vision war shirt?"

Chapter 3

The Shirt Recovery Party

I had never seen my friends so excited as they were when Charlie Conrad told them he had seen Bear Chief's war shirt. At last we were to learn who had stolen it. "How wonderful! Sun himself caused this to happen!" they cried. Bear Chief was trembling, giving thanks to Sun. I pulled him down beside me, quieted the others, and Conrad said to us:

"It was sometime back. A large number of riders, with many loose horses, came to the front of my store, and I went out to meet them, to invite them to sit and smoke with me. I had never seen any of them before, but as they were without saddles, many carrying bows and arrows, I knew they were a war party of some foreign tribe on their way to hunt our buffalo and steal our horses. One of them, who seemed to be their leader, was wearing a war shirt. He signed to me that they had not time to sit and smoke, but had a few beaver skins they wanted to trade for cartridges and tobacco. Five of them came in, the others remaining outside to take care of the horses. As I traded with them, I kept looking at the war shirt; at the many holes cut in it; at the darker patch of buckskin on its right sleeve. By those holes and by the different colored patch I was sure the war shirt belonged to my friend Bear Chief. I feared that its wearer had killed him, but I kept that thought to myself, signing to the man: "Very good, your war shirt. Where did you get it?"

"I made it; long ago I made it," he answered. I then asked him to give me the name of his tribe, and he signed: "We are members of the Spotted Horses People (Cheyenne). But from the sly smiles and looks of several of his party, I knew that he had lied to me. Ha! Just then entered a white man who had come up river on one of the steamboats; at once he began talking with the five in their own language. I saw that they were not glad to meet him; they quickly finished trading with me, hurried out to their horses, and rode away. I then asked the white man to tell me who they were. Laughing, he answered: "Their leader, the one in the war shirt, begged me not to tell you that, but I will. They are Cut Throats (Assiniboines). My home is at Wolf Point, where I have traded with them during many winters."

"*Hai-ya! Hai-ya!* Cut Throats! Our most lasting enemies!" Bear Chief exclaimed.

"True. But always we have so fought them that they have failed to take for themselves any of our great country," said Old Bull.

"Well, Bear Chief, how did that man manage to steal your war shirt?" Conrad asked.

"With my war bonnet and shield it was on a tripod close behind my lodge. Came evening, and my Sits-Beside-Me Woman went to bring them in for the night. Lo! The war shirt was gone, right in daytime stolen, and none noticed the coming and going of the thief," my friend answered.

"Ha! He is crazy-brave, that one. Well, that downriver white man told me the Cut Throat is a chief of his people, and that his name is Sitting Eagle," said Conrad.

Said Bear Chief: "Spotted Fur Cap, tell me about the thief as you remember him."

"Not old; perhaps forty winters. He is tall and strong bodied; he has long hair and a nose like an eagle's bill; he has a scar on his right cheek."

"Ha! By that scar I shall know him. Spotted Fur Cap, see how Sun helps us his children: He planned that I should learn from you about the thief." Then after a pause, he went on solemnly: "All of you, my friends here, listen! This I vow: I shall do my utmost to find Sitting Eagle and recover my war shirt. I shall kill him, or be killed by him!" Then he added to me: "Come, Apikuni, let us find my women before they trade all of our furs for women's articles."

This was a sad breach of etiquette, as it was always up to the host to ceremoniously dismiss a smoking party by knocking out the ashes of the pipe and exclaiming: *Kyi! Itsinitsi!* There! Burned out!" But Conrad took it in good part, lightly saying that a smoking party must never delay a warrior from getting at his enemy.

We found the women outside, standing by their laden horses, and Bear Chief said to them: "I am glad that you haven't traded, for I want many cartridges."

"But you have some back in our lodge," Fox Woman offered.

"I know that, but I need still more for what I am to do. Listen, you women! We have just now learned from Spotted Fur Hat that my war shirt was stolen by a Cut Throat named Sitting Eagle, a chief. Well, I am going to get it back from him, and Apikuni, here, is one of those who will go with me."

"Kyai-ya! Kyai-ya!" the women wailed. "A Cut Throat the thief! Bear Chief, go not in quest of him — he is so

31

powerful!" And said I: "No, my friend, I go not with any war party." But he laughed and said to them: "Well he knows he has to go to war, accomplish some brave deed before he can really be one of us, a real Pikuni." Right then and there I knew I was, at last, to be a member of a war party.

Though there were five clerks in the store, it was long before we could get to one of them with our buffalo robes and furs, of which I had two beaver hides, seven mink hides, and three fox hides, the result of my spring trapping. I traded them for some clothing, shoes, tobacco, and cartridges. Bear Chief took two hundred cartridges and some tobacco, but left the rest of the trading to his wives. For about four hundred dollars worth of furs they received large supplies of sugar, tea, coffee, flour, blankets, dress goods, and various other necessities. But their purchases brought them no happiness: their man was going to war, perhaps never to return to them. They were silent all the way back to camp.

That evening many of the leading men of the camp gathered in our lodge to discuss the great news of the day, Spotted Fur Cap's disclosure of the identity of the war shirt thief. They wondered that any one could be so crazy-brave as to enter our active camp and walk off with the shirt. Was it, Big Swan ventured, that this Sitting Eagle enemy had some kind of secret power making him invisible to those of us who all day long had been passing near Bear Chief's sacred articles on the tripod back of his lodge? Well, that war shirt was probably now on the way to the Camp of the Cut Throats at Wolf Point (Mahkwiyi Piskatchis) or somewhere in between. To take it from the thief would be difficult, almost impossible.

Said Bear Chief in reply to this idea: "Difficult, I know. But Sun is powerful. I have a feeling, a strong belief, that

32

He will help me take back my war shirt and make that Sitting Eagle unable ever to sit again. I shall want a few of my friends to go with me in quest of it. Apikuni, here, is one of them."

Many of our circle shouted that they would go, but Bear Chief said he would need only a few to accompany him, and would name them later on. Then his wives and several of the old men chanted, half-sang: "Apikuni! Ha! Apikuni, ho! Apikuni is brave! Good it is that Apikuni will make our enemies to cry!" Then Bear Chief, noting my embarrassment, knocked the ashes from his pipe, saying it was burned out, whereupon our friends left, and I took to my couch. Wolf Point! I well remembered it — on the north side of the Missouri and thirty or forty miles below the mouth of Milk River. The *Far West* had stopped there to take on wood. Near the landing was a large trading post built of logs, and lining the shore, a throng of Indians had stood staring at the boat, at us, some of them spitting at us, shouting, and signing that they hated us. They were, the captain told us, some of the Yankton Sioux, who, after taking part in killing General Custer and his men the year before, had sneaked north to live with their brother tribe, the Assiniboine, pretending they were members of it.

For two days Bear Chief kept much to himself as he considered which of his friends he would ask to join his party. On both days I rode to town to chat with friends. Family after family of our camp also went in to town, to do some last trading and to sit and stare at the steamboats. *'Istsi' awkiosahchists*, fire boats they called them, most wonderful of all the white man's creations. For the boats had life — keen eyes to watch the river ahead and so to travel in its deepest part. The boats were being loaded with bales of buffalo robes, and with deer, elk, wolf, an-

33

telope, and beaver hides, the result of the winter trades. Charlie Conrad told me that ten thousand buffalo robes, tanned mostly by women of the Blackfeet tribes, had been shipped in the late spring, during high water, by the town's traders. The Indians received, on an average, five dollars worth of trade goods for each buffalo robe, which in the States sold at from twenty-five to fifty dollars each — they were used as sleigh and carriage robes.

On my last day in town, Charlie Conrad called me into his office and said: "I have just heard that Bear Chief is organizing a war party to get back his war shirt and that you are to be a member."

"Yes, he asked me to go. I couldn't refuse."

"You mean you didn't want to refuse; you want to go. Well now, my boy, I know how exciting it is, the life you are having with the Pikuni: hunting with them; learning their language, their religious beliefs; taking part in all of their strange and interesting social activities. All well enough for a time, but you just can't keep on with it. And as to going to war with them —no, no! What would your mother, your relatives, and your friends think if they knew? White men do not join Indians in their intertribal fights."

"Jim Bridger, Kit Carson, and other old timers did," I responded.

"Yes, but they had good reason; they were forced to do so. You must not go with this Bear Chief war party. It is too dangerous. You might be killed."

"Well, I'll think about it," I shortly answered. I then hurried out, mounted my horse, and rode back to camp, having fully decided I would be one of the war party.

Tired and hungry, I unsaddled my horse, turned it loose, and entered the lodge. Fox Woman fed me. Bear Chief was happily singing a war song, beating time with

34

his drum. He ended, saying to me: "Well, Apikuni, our war party is made up. We are to be eight men: Last Rider, White Antelope, Little Otter, Heavy Runner, Owl Child, Old Bull, you, and I. Tomorrow Red Eagle's woman will build a sweat lodge for us, he will pray for us, and then we will start out upon our sacred quest. Many men have come to me, wanting to join our party. Of these I have chosen only six — all have proved brave and are close friends."

True enough — they were Bear Chief's close friends. They had made many raids on enemy camps, as evidenced by the large bands of enemy horses they had; by the enemy scalps with which their war shirts were fringed. Of the six, I liked Old Bull best; in fact, I revered him. He was a man of about forty winters — tall and well muscled, with long hair, keen eyes, and a pleasant face; calm, dignified, and honest; moreover, he was a sacred pipe man, a medicine man, as the whites say. Old Bull was possessor of the powerful Eagle Head pipe, master of its long ritual of sacred prayers and songs.

Soon after sunset, our six friends came in to sit and smoke with us and learn Bear Chief's plan for our difficult undertaking. We would, he said, cross Big River (the Missouri) at Many Houses (Fort Benton) and go down the south side of the river valley until, near the mouth of Little River (Milk River), we would recross Big River, in case we were required to go as far as Wolf Point. It was well known that enemy war parties traveled more frequently north of the river than they did south of it. We would, of course, go on foot and travel only at night.

Said Little Otter: "Such a long way to go on foot. I think we should ride."

Bear Chief answered forcefully: "Were we going just to raid an enemy camp to take some horses, I would favor going on horseback and risk meeting an enemy war party.

35

But, my friends, what we are setting out to do is different; in order to recover my war shirt we must take no risk we can possibly avoid. So is it that we go on foot and as secretly as possible."

At this point I put in: "Friends, I know a better way to go, an easier way: I will buy a boat in Many Houses, and we will go down river in it."

"Yes! Yes!" "Good! Good" "Hai-ya! That is how we should go," cried Last Rider, Little Otter, and White Antelope. But frowning and raising his hand in protest, Bear Chief growled: "Are you three crazy? Can't you see how wrong you are? Were we to boat-ride down river in daytime, soon some enemy war party on shore would shoot us. And you know the white men's fire boats, though strong their eyes, dare not travel at night lest they strike rocks or other obstacles and so get torn apart. Were we, in a small boat, to nightride down, we would soon strike something that would upset us and cause us at the least to lose our guns."

"Yes, and we would probably then be seized and killed by the terrible Water People," Old Bull tersely added. At this comment, Last Rider and Owl Child visibly shuddered. The Blackfeet firmly believed that all large rivers and lakes are inhabited by a human-like monster race — *Suyi Tupiks*, Water People, who frequently seize land swimmers, kill them, and take them down to their under-water lodges. In the very-long-ago, Blackfeet ancestors had seen this done.

"Well, so it is that we night-travel, and on foot," said Bear Chief. Furthermore, I have asked old Red Eagle to give us a going-away sweat lodge ceremony tomorrow afternoon, for his sacred Thunder Bird ritual is powerful. I know his prayer for us will be helpful. Then, after he finishes with us, we will take up our belongings and go upon our quest." And with that our meeting ended.

Early on the following morning, I hurriedly rode to town to ask Gus Senor, carpenter and boat builder, to ferry us across the river some time that evening. Of course, I had to tell him who we were, a party of eight going to recover Bear Chief's war shirt. At this news, Senor stared at me glumly, shook his head, but merely said: "All right, I'll do it. Call on me when you're ready, and five dollars will be about right." I gave him the money and sped back to camp.

In mid-morning Red Eagle's four wives began making the sweat lodges we were to use. They cut a number of extra long slender willows, trimmed off the branches, except the tips; then, in small holes dug in the ground, they set the butts to make a circle about twelve feet in diameter; in the center of the circle they dug a shallow depression about two feet in diameter; they then brought together the tips of the willows, securely tied them, and covered the framework with pieces of old lodge leather. Made in this way, the lodge had the shape of a semi-sphere. On top, a buffalo skull wreathed with sprays of sweet sage, was placed, a symbol of meat, the staff of life, and thus a token of success.

The lodge completed, the women rested until mid-afternoon, when they built a fire and began heating some stones. Then members of the Bear Chief war party took off their clothing, wrapped themselves in blankets, and waited Red Eagle's call. In due time the call came, and one after another we entered the lodge. Red Eagle, naked, was sitting at the west side of the lodge, awaiting us. We thrust our blankets out under the lodge covering, where they would remain dry, and naked, we sat in a circle in the dim light of the lodge. Soon the women, with wooden tongs, began passing in red-hot stones from their fire, and

37

OLD BULL ON CROW HORSE (Esa-Po-Me-Ta)
by Glen Eagle Speaker

Old Bull, also with tongs, piled them in the hollowed out center place. Set before Red Eagle was a wooden bowl filled with water, and when the stones were all in place, he dipped a buffalo tail into the water and began sprinkling the stones; as dense steam spread and filled the lodge, he sang a prayer to Sun for help in our undertaking, in which we all joined, perspiration streaming from our bodies.

Occasionally sprinkling the hot stones to keep the lodge full of steam, Red Eagle prayed to Sun, to his wife Moon, to their son Morning Star, and to Seven Persons (constellation of Ursa Major) to keep us safe from all enemies, to give us success in our quest for the war shirt, and for a full and happy life to old age. The songs were interspersed with prayers, and during every prayer and every song, we repeatedly brought our folded hands against our breasts and bowed our heads in reverence to the Above Ones. The music of the songs, all in minor key, were fully as classic, as profound, as are the symphonies of Mendelssohn, Handel, and Mozart. Anyone who attends, in any July, the Sun Lodge ceremonies of any Blackfeet tribe, can hear this music and these songs, and the prayers of the Blackfeet Sun Priests, so-called medicine men.

The ceremony lasted all of two hours. At last the end came, when one after another we knelt before Red Eagle while he painted our faces and hands with red ochre, Sun's sacred color, as he named us, prayed for us. We then reached out for our blankets, and wrapped in them, we hurried to the river, bathed, and returned to our lodges to dress and prepare to leave. The sun was setting when we all gathered before Bear Chief's Lodge. Bear Chief then addressed us: "Well, my brave ones, are you sure you have everything you need, that you haven't forgotten this or that necessity? Good! We go!" And with that he led off. All the people of the camp stood silently before their lodges to watch us leave, no wife or mother daring to cry lest she cause bad luck for her dear one. We were soon out from camp, heading for Fort Benton, just over the ridge.

Our weapons were 1873 Winchester repeating rifles, for which we each had two hundred or more cartridges in belts around our waists. Our accessories were many, but light: slung from our shoulders were buckskin or parfleche sacks containing two or three pairs of moccasins; awl and sinew thread for repairing them; various face paints; comb and small mirror; tobacco and kakisin, dried leaves of partridgeberry plants for mixing with tobacco; and for our next meal some roasted meat. Most important, for future use, we each had a braided, pliable rawhide lariat. Old Bull carried his sacred Eagle Head pipe, since he was to be our prophet; by his visions he would foretell danger ahead, so that we might be watchful and avoid it. My friends all wore moccasins, leggings, breechclouts, shirts of buckskin, and blanket capotes, carrying their war bonnets in parfleche cases. I wore underwear, shoes, socks, woolen shirt, trousers and jacket, and a broad-brim hat; most precious of all, in my war sack were the two volumes of the Lewis and Clark Expedition of 1804-06, published by Harper and Brother. I had read them many times. I also carried a small telescope, which my mother had given me as I entered Peekskill Military Academy. Now I was to travel down a stretch of the Missouri River valley which Lewis and Clark had so laboriously ascended in 1805, describing their daily adventures in minute detail. To my mind, the greatest and most important of all exploratory expeditions was the Lewis and Clark expedition up the Missouri and on to the Pacific Coast and back. Of course, we all had butcher knives and handled steels for sharpening them, and Last Rider and White

40

Antelope each had a medium sized hatchet.

We made the three miles to Fort Benton quickly, pausing on its one business street, which faced the river. Bear Chief observed: "Where is the boat we are to cross in? Where is it tied?"

"Just below that fireboat," I answered, pointing to the lowest one of three at the levee.

"Because of the bright night, we must separate to go to it. Were we to go together, any of the white soldiers from the fort happening to see us would know we are a war party and would make trouble for us. As you know, that soldier chief Underground Mouse (Colonel Edward A. Moale, Third Infantry, U.S.A.) says that your-and-our Grandfather (President of the United States) has ordered him to seize all war parties and make them return to their camp." Just at this time, however, the army, due to the recent Custer massacre, was hesitant to enforce these orders. At almost any other time, the army would have ordered or escorted the Assiniboine war party, including Sitting Eagle, back to the reservation at Wolf Point.

The big adobe fort was well to our left. One by one we crossed the street and gathered at the boat, but Senor was not there. Leaving my rifle, cartridge belts, and war sack, I went in search of him. He was not at home, but I finally found him playing faro in Keno Bill's saloon. He looked up at me, nodded, cashed in his checks. Said the faro dealer: "Why quit, Gus? You are winning plenty." He answered that he would be back. Keno Bill, behind the bar, called to us: "Here, you two, have a drink."

Gus accepted, but I was not a whiskey drinker. Bill looked at me, frowning, and said: "I know what you are up to, young fellow. My wife's brother, Last Rider, told us the whole story. Well, all I have to say is that you watch your step! Plumb dangerous, what you are setting out to do!

Now then, you stay at my house tonight, and in the morning I'll take you back to camp."

"Yes, you do that!" Senor urged.

I silently signed to him: "I have to go!"

We came to my friends at the boat, and Old Bull said: "So it is that we really go." Then tossing a piece of plug smoking tobacco into the river, he chanted forcefully: *"Haiyu! Haiyu Suyi Tupiks! Kituhguk pistakan. Kitak ochisop. Nitak opmo anan. Kimoket anan. Pinut kimutsi stutoki anan."* Correctly translated, this was what he said: "Listen! Listen, Water People. I give you tobacco. You are to smoke. Pity us. We are to cross over. Do not harm us."

We then boarded the boat, and I helped Senor row. After we landed, he remained in the boat, and I rowed it upstream a way, so that in recrossing, he could easily make his landing place. Then we said brief goodbyes, whereupon I hurried back to my friends. Wordlessly we started down the river valley, Bear Chief in the lead.

Chapter 4

Fort Benton to Fort Claggett

We soon waded across Box Alder Creek, called Shonkin Creek by the whites. Through grove after grove of cottonwood and across long stretches of grassy bottom land we kept on and on during the night. Twice, where the river flowed deeply against high cliffs, we had to climb to the plain above to be able to travel on. The eastern sky was reddening when we arrived in a small grove directly opposite the mouth of Marias River, commonly pronounced as though spelled "Mayryeass," with the accent on the second syllable. It is the Marias River of Lewis and Clark's Journal, Captain Lewis having named it for his cousin Miss Maria Wood, on June 8, 1805. The Blackfeet tribes' name for it is *Kyai Isisakta*, Bear River.

Hurriedly undressing, we bathed in the river, dressed and then ate some of the roasted meat we carried in our war sacks. Bear Chief called on Last Rider and White Antelope to go up on to the rim of the plain to watch for enemies. At noon he was to send Little Otter and Owl Child to relieve them. Old Bull, our Sun's man, or medicine man as the whites have it, went from us a little way to pray to the Above Ones to give him a revealing vision as he slept alone, and we five others were soon asleep. I slept so soundly that I did not hear Bear Chief change the watch. The sun was setting when Old Bull came and awakened us and when the watchers came down from the rim of the plain, saying they had seen no signs of enemies. Old Bull gruffly observed that his sleep had been visionless. At that we went to the river and drank, then ate the last of our roasted meat. As we resumed our way down the valley, Bear Chief remarked that, come daylight, we would have to kill some kind of meat animal and roast enough to last several days.

The moon and stars gave so much light that we had no difficulty in traveling through one after another of the groves of the valley, and in the prairie-like stretches we made fast time. When dawn came, I thought we had traveled all of twenty miles. Full daylight came as we were making our way in an extensive grove. As we neared its lower edge, Bear Chief slowed us, signing that we go cautiously, then brought us to a halt, and pointing, spoke with quiet reverence: "The Above Ones favor us; they bring us to real-food *(nitapi waksin)* as we need it." Sure enough, there at the river's edge, not a hundred yards away, three buck whitetail deer were drinking. Whispered Old Bull as they one by one turned back into the open to pass before us: "One of us should do the killing. Bear Chief, name him!"

"Nistoa — I," he hissed. He shot the lead buck, and as the other two were running past us, downed them both. He then told Heavy Runner and Little Otter to go up to the rim of the plain to watch the surrounding country until mid-day, when they would be relieved.

Happily singing a song of plenty, Old Bull sat down, filled his little pipe (his big sacred Eagle Head pipe was only for ceremonial use), and watched us butcher the deer

44

while he smoked. It was not for him, our sacred prophet, to do work of any kind. We were his servants: we cooked his food, brought him water and carried some of his belongings as we traveled. Bear Chief asked what parts of the deer we should broil for him. "The tongues, and thin cuttings of the fattest of the meat," Old Bull answered.

Having finished the butchering, we built a long fire of smokeless wood and broiled enough of the meat to last for several days, at the same time feeding Old Bull and ourselves. We then slept, Old Bull somewhere off by himself. All too soon, I thought, Bear Chief gave me a poke in the ribs and said: "Come, we must relieve our tired and hungry watchers."

We found them in a stand of greasewood at the edge of the plain. They had seen no sign whatever of enemies. They went swiftly down the slope, and Bear Chief said to me: "You are so young and worn out — you must lie down and sleep. When Sun is halfway from mid-day to His setting, you shall watch and I will sleep." I told him he was generous and kind, and I was asleep as soon as I stretched out in the brush.

It was, I thought, all of five o'clock when he wakened me to take the watch. Sleepily I sat up, rubbing my eyes as he stretched out with his war sack for a pillow. I swayed as I sat, closed my eyes, and almost slept again. But that would not do — on me now depended the safety of my friends, of myself. Keenly I began scanning the river valley and the great plain for the least sign of danger. Out to the south were a few bands of antelope, some grazing, others at rest. After a time a big wolf came to the rim of the plain, several hundred yards west of us, and gave some of his long-drawn, melancholy, and far-reaching howls. Down in the valley several of his kind answered his calls. Again and again at intervals he howled, and at last

45

five other wolves joined him, males, for at that time of year the females were denned with their young, the males taking to them the meat their families needed. One by one as they came, the five and the caller, wagging their tails, smelled of one another. Then they trotted out onto the plain, the caller in the lead. He had gathered them for an antelope chase, the young animals to be easily overtaken and killed.

Although the howling of wolves, yelping of coyotes, and muffled barking of foxes may seem never to vary in length or in time, apparently there are subtle differences which indicate the animals' activities: a call for a hunt, the announcement of new found meat, or a warning of danger.

The sun was near setting when, down at our camp, a rifle was fired and then came more shots as I awakened Bear Chief and yelled: "They are fighting down there." Snatching up our rifles and belongings, we ran down the steep slope of the valley, but as we went, heard no more shots, no yells. At the foot of the slope, we paused, Bear Chief saying: "I don't know what to think of this — there was enough shooting for our friends to be all killed."

"No more than six or seven shots," I put in.

Slowly and watchfully we went on into the timber, soon sighting our friends whom we had heard talking and laughing as they sat around a fire roasting more meat. Cried Bear Chief as we hurried to them: "That shooting — what happened?"

Up sprang Little Otter, who turned, pointed and answered: "Off there, *Nitap okaiyo* ("real bear," or grizzly) nearly got me!" He led us to the huge, light-furred female that would, I thought, weigh all of eight hundred pounds. As he began cutting off her long sharp claws, he said that, wanting more deer meat, he had hunted at the edge of the grove and had come upon three young cubs. Bawling, they

46

had run toward their mother, who was feasting on the remains of one of our deer. As she charged him, he had fired twice, wounding her both times, but she had kept coming and would have reached him had not Old Bull and the others hurried to his assistance and killed her.

"Well, Little Otter, you will not have a real-bear-claws necklace to wear," I said.

"No. As I did not alone kill the she one, I could not wear it. When I make it, I will give it to Sun, praying Him for long and full life for us all," he answered. He would tie it to a tree limb, sacrificing it to Sun with much prayer. In this way the Blackfeet tribes gave away many of their choicest possessions.

As we broiled and ate our evening meal of deer meat, I sprinkled my portion with the condiments I had. Bear Chief remarked, as he had several times before, that the whites had some strange habits, one of them the dusting of their food with tastes-like-fire *(istsi powki)* and tastes-like-tobacco, pepper tobacco *(aipistakwi pokwi)*. I smiled, telling him that in the far south there were tribes of Indians who used salt, had always used it. They could not be real Indians, he thought.

White Antelope began telling a funny story, but Old Bull raised a warning hand, signed him to be silent, and gravely said to us: "My brave ones, I have to tell you that as I slept, I was given a warning vision. As I, my shadow, was walking in the valley of a little stream, I heard women wailing for a dear dead person; going a little farther, I saw them, four women, their faces black-painted, sitting under a tree in the limbs of which they had lashed the robe-wrapped body of their dear one. Suddenly I awoke and could not sleep again. As you all know, such a vision is a warning from the Above Ones of danger somewhere ahead."

47

"Ha! Plain enough your warning vision," Last Rider interrupted. "Right after you had it, the she real-bear attacked me!"

Said Bear Chief: "I never heard of a vision that gave warning of bears or any other four footed ones."

Old Bull exclaimed, "Visions warn us only of men enemies somewhere about; we must see them before they see us, and plan what to do."

"True, True! Let us go on, more than ever watchful," replied Bear Chief.

Silently we took up our belongings and in the deepening dusk resumed our way down the valley. As we neared the deer carcasses, we heard the bear cubs go bawling away. The valley was now an ever-narrowing canyon, its sides high cliffs of fantastic shape. Soon we came to a bend of the river where, deep below a cliff, it blocked our way. Again we had to climb up to the plain and keep well out on it to avoid the many coulees along the edge. When morning came, we were still out on the plain, several miles from the breaks of *Apsi isisakta*, Arrow River of the Blackfeet and Arrow Creek of the whites. The Blackfeet named it after a large bed of flint near its source, where they had often made arrow and spear points.

With Old Bull's warning vision in mind, we paused often to look carefully for any signs of enemies, but everywhere bands of antelope were grazing, resting, or going leisurely to and from their watering places. We came to the brink of the creek valley, narrow and sparsely timbered. Up and down the valley and right in front of us, deer and antelope were quietly moving about, evidence that no enemies were near. Bear Chief told Little Otter and Heavy Runner to sit and watch the area for a time, and we hurried down to the creek, drank, and in a small grove ate some of our roasted deer meat, before stretching out to rest. Bear Chief then went back alone to relieve the watchers. Returning at noon, he had Owl Child take the afternoon watch.

Somehow we did not sleep well and were all up and bathing in the creek some hours before sunset; we then gathered to smoke. Old Bull remarked that he was worried — he had had no vision; therefore, his warning vision of the night before still held, of danger somewhere ahead.

For the first time on our journey I took out my volume of the Lewis and Clark expedition, and after reading a certain part, I said: "My friends, I am going to tell you about this thick-writing of two soldier chiefs. They, with thirty soldiers and other men, were the first whites ever to come up Big River. That was seventy-five summers ago. One of the men, a Nothing-White-Man, had with him his Snake wife, her name Bird Woman."

"Yes, yes, our people heard about them from the Entrails People. Those whites killed two of them," Bear Chief interrupted. The Blackfeet name for the French is *Kistap Apikwaks*, Nothing, or Worthless-White men. Charbonneau, the husband of Bird Woman, was French.

Said Old Bull: "My mother knew that Bird Woman. she met her in Many Houses (Fort Benton)."

This surprised me. I was later to learn that many Pikuni women knew her.

"Those whites came upriver with two large boats and six small ones," I continued, "and every night the two soldier chiefs wrote of the distance they had traveled during the day, and of all they had seen and done. On the day they passed the mouth of Arrow River, they found, a little way below it, at the foot of a cliff on the north side of Big River, the remains of more than a hundred buffalo that Indians had frightened off the cliff. Nearby had been their camp of one hundred and twenty-five lodges. The

49

soldier chiefs wrote that this encampment must have been of a tribe of the Parted Hairs (Sioux) named Minnetares, which, I understand, means Water People."

"Ha! There the soldier chiefs made a big mistake," Old Bull exclaimed. "Never has any tribe of the Parted Hairs dared to come into our country to camp and live permanently on our buffalo herds. Without doubt the camp site they saw was one of our Blackfeet tribes." And to that Bear Chief and the others gave loud assent.

"Well, because they found buffalo remains at the foot of the cliff, the soldier chiefs named this stream Slaughter Creek," I said.

"Matters not what those whites named it. This is our very own Arrow River!" Old Bull growled.

"Well, friends, we must now be not far from the westernmost herds of the buffalo," I offered.

"True! True! We will soon be eating buffalo tongues, dorsal ribs, stuffed entrails!" said White Antelope, and we all grinned and smacked our lips.

From reports of some of our war parties, of steamboat men, and of Indian Agents and others, we knew that from Canada south to far beyond the Yellowstone River, and from the eastern part of the Blackfeet country on into the country of the Parted Hair tribes (North Dakota), buffalo herds were said to be as plentiful as ever. We had talked of this several times, and of a friend, Ahsakwi (Brown), who had a trading post at the mouth of Yellow River (Judith), living there with his Pikuni wife, his children, and his brother-in-law Owns-His-Own-Horses. The whites' name for Ahsakwi was Diamond R. Brown, as for some years he had been the "wagon boss" (foreman) of the Diamond R. bull train, owned by Broadwater and Pepin, traders at Fort Assiniboine and owners of a great herd of cattle branded with an eight sided figure with the letter "R" in

50

the center.

Diamond R. Brown was dark complexioned, and much of the time he dressed and looked like an Indian. Letting his hair grow long, he braided it, often wearing two eagle feathers in the braids. The Indians seemed to like him for his Indian style, and I am sure that dressing as an Indian increased his trading activity tremendously.

Bear Chief now said, "*Kyi*, my brave ones. We will not return to Big River to continue this night's travel. Instead, we will go straight ahead on the plain to the mouth of Yellow River and there have a smoke with Brown before going on down Big River."

We all gave quick assent to his idea and were soon on our way, fording the creek and climbing up onto the plain just as the sun was setting. So it was that we had a good view of the Wolf Mountains, *Mahkwi Istukists* of the Blackfeet, the Little Rockies of the whites, twenty miles or more north of the Missouri. At the eastern end of the range is a high bare-sided butte, its summit a dense grove of pines. This imposing butte, a favorite lookout place of war parties, was long ago named *Imuyis Tsimokan* (Hairy Hat) by the Blackfeet. Also, to the south, we could plainly see the *Otokwi istukists* (Yellow Mountains) and the *Kwun Istukists*, Snow Mountains of the Blackfeet tribes, the Judith and the Snowy Mountains of the whites.

As we stood enjoying the superb view, my friends with pleasant memories of camping and hunting around in this area, we saw, though far away and dimly, three huge dark-colored animals come up onto the plain from the breaks of the Missouri, and as one man we shouted: *"Inuah! Inuah! Inuah!"* Buffalo! Buffalo! Buffalo! Bear Chief adding: *"Stumikikis! Niokskum!"* Bulls! Three!

"Let us kill one of them! Come on!" Heavy Runner urged.

51

"No! They are a sure sign that there are plenty of buffalo ahead, and we have enough meat for our morning meal," Old Bull objected, and after a last careful scrutiny for signs of enemies, we started on. My friends were keeping well in mind Old Bull's vision of danger for us, somewhere ahead. My own thought was that, vision or no vision, we were in constant danger of being surprise-attacked by a prowling war party. At that time of year, war parties of the Crows, Crees, Cheyennes, Cut Throats, and Sioux infested our country, seeking, at no great risk to themselves, Blackfeet horses and Blackfeet scalps.

Our shining time keeper, Seven Persons, let us know that it was near midnight when, from the rim of the plain, we looked down at the large grassy and partly timbered bottom land through which Yellow River (Judith) gently flowed to join Big River (Missouri). Well above the junction and close to the latter stream, we could plainly see Fort Claggett: a long wide log house, log stable, and corrals. Said Little Otter: "Well, there it is, our friend Brown's trading house. We will soon be smoking with him and his good woman. Ermine Woman will give us plenty to drink and eat, as she has always done on other visits."

"No, we have no right to waken them this late at night," I objected. "They need their sleep, and we need sleep too, as we had but little of it at Arrow River yesterday. Let us lie down close in front of their house, giving them a surprise when they come out in the morning."

Said Bear Chief: "Apikuni is right. We must not waken them. Come on, we will rest close to their house."

We crossed the wide bottom, stole past the big house, stopped in front of the corrals, in which were a number of horses, Bear Chief telling us to lie down and sleep, saying he would sit up and watch. One of the corrals contained only the horses trained by Diamond R.'s brother-in-law

52

for buffalo hunting. The other contained only one horse, Diamond R.'s favorite, a beautiful Appaloosa, which I had admired and delighted in each time I had seen him. It was some time before I slept, as I lay thinking of Lewis' and Clark's discovery of the Judith River on May 29, 1805. They had ascended for a mile and a half and had seen along its breaks great numbers of *argali*, their name for bighorn sheep. Captain Clark had named the stream for his sweetheart, Miss Julia Hancock, of Fincastle, Virginia, whom he married in 1808 and who died in 1820. He always called her Judie, thinking her name a shortening of Judith. Just above the confluence of the two rivers, the explorers had found a recently abandoned Indian camp site of 126 lodges. On examining some discarded moccasins, their guide, Sacajawea, Bird Woman, had said that they were not moccasins of her tribe, the Shoshoni, but were probably those of a tribe living on this side of the Rocky Mountains and north of the Missouri. Why, I wondered, had she not said that it had been a camp of a Blackfeet tribe, for it was in the heart of their great country, as she well knew. Lewis and Clark had written that the camp had probably been that of the Minnetares from Fort de Prairie! And thus musing, I finally slept.

Suddenly Bear Chief was quietly waking us, reporting that enemies had come — they were in the corral that contained the buffalo horses. They were roping the snorting milling horses and making an opening in the corral for a getaway. We would, he whispered, go around and first shoot those opening the corral, then those inside. The smaller corral was empty, the one that had held R. Brown's Appaloosa, stolen first. Cautiously we stole along the east side of the corral, keeping close to it. When we rounded the corner, we saw, close ahead, two men frantically pulling out the long pine poles of a panel. Bear Chief,

Old Bull, and Heavy Runner, who were in the lead, fired, and both enemies fell, one with piercing shrieks of pain. At that we all climbed to the top of the corral, looking for enemies within it, shooting at the few we could see among the wildly panicking horses. The enemy raiders occasionally shot at us as they made for the west side of the corral to climb out and flee. I shot at a climber and shouted as he fell: "I killed him! I killed that tall one!" But Last Rider, close at my left, just as loudly yelled: "You did not! I killed him, shot him in the middle of his back!"

The horses were now jumping over the knee-high poles remaining in the opened panel and running off across the grassy flat. The shooting ended. Little Otter, sitting and swaying from side to side, summoned us: "Help me — I am shot!"

Diamond R., Owns-His-Own-Horses, and Ermine Woman came hurrying to us, they in their night clothes and with rifles in hand, Ermine Woman shrilly crying as she embraced her relative Heavy Runner: "Oh, how the shooting frightened us, and how happy we were when we heard you Pikuni shouting to one another!"

"Yes. And you saved many of our horses," Diamond R. added. He understood and spoke the *nitapi powaksin*, the real Blackfeet language.

Chapter 5

At Diamond R. Brown's

As motherly Ermine Woman knelt to help wounded Little Otter, we others scattered to examine our kills, Last Rider and I hurrying to the one we both claimed. He got there first, snatched up the dead one's rifle, a rimfire Henry, and shouted: "I killed this enemy. I take his gun as proof of it!"

"But look! He is not back-shot," I all but yelled, pointing to the dead man, his face and breast against the ground, his thin shirt bloodless, but the top of his head a bloody mess.

In turn, Last Rider stared down at the man and visibly sagged. "Oh, true, true," he wailed. "I can't count coup on him. Maybe neither of us killed him, but anyhow I will keep his gun."

"And I will take what he was carrying, whatever it is," I said, lifting a painted, fringed cylindrical parfleche case slung from the corpse's shoulder, later to find that it contained a beautiful war bonnet of eagle tail-feathers.

There were three other dead enemies in the corral, which with the two at the broken panel, made a total of six. Also, there were two dead horses, and one wounded. I ended the latter's pain, then asked Bear Chief who our enemies were.

"Why surely you should know that," he exclaimed. "Their hair is parted in the middle, a braid falling in front of each ear, and the designs of their quilled moccasins, of pyramids and triangles, are sure proof that they are Assiniboines."

I noticed that our kills were tall, well muscled men, that their hair braids were long, and that their soft tanned buckskin shirts and leggings were beautifully decorated with bead and quill work. One was a heavy-set man, who wore his hair tied behind in a thick queue and cut short in front; in his ears he had strings of white glass beads; around his neck was a collar of bear claws. Close inspection left no doubt that these people were indeed Assinibones.

The sun was rising as we turned from the corral, and Ermine Woman said to us: "You brave ones, I am now going to cook for you, and real-food it is going to be."

"Yes. A small herd of buffalo was in the bottom yesterday, and I killed one, a fat two winters' cow," Ahsakwi added.

Then Ermine Woman continued: "Oh, you brave ones, I can't wait to learn how you happen to have come here just in time to save our horses, and probably us, from those terrible Cut Throats."

We looked to Bear Chief to answer her. Briefly he said: "A Cut Throat named Sitting Eagle stole my war shirt. We are on our way to kill Sitting Eagle and recover my shirt."

"We will tell you about it later," Old Bull put in.

Before going in for the feast, we paused to look off at the long wide bottom land at the junction of the two rivers. Nearby, twenty-five or thirty horses were hungrily grazing. We had to guess where the surviving Cut Throats might be, perhaps in the timber lining Yellow River, or sneaking up the river on their way home. It would have been dangerous to look for them in the timber, where they would have had every advantage over us.

We went to the river and bathed, combing our hair; my friends painted themselves, and we entered Ahsakwi's big living room, where Old Bull sat filling a pipe for us to smoke. Ermine Woman was at a big cookstove, and the odor of boiling meat and coffee made us hungrier than ever. Sitting at my side, Ahsakwi said: "It is for you and me to put those dead Assiniboines where they won't stink, but first I'll get rid of the dead horses. I'll hitch up a team and drag them off; then with a wagon we'll do the rest of the work."

I nodded my head, said that I was all for it. The men of the Blackfeet tribes took no part in the funeral rituals for their dead, or even for those dearest to them — their wives, children, parents. It fell to the women to robe-wrap the dead and lash them to platforms of poles which they set in branches of trees, there in time the body would disintegrate in the elements or fall to predators.

We had a royal feast of boiled buffalo *issuists* — hump ribs; yeast bread; sugared coffee; and dried apple sauce. While we ate, Bear Chief told our hosts in detail of the theft of his war shirt, and how, by the Sun's great help, the thief's identity had been made known to us by close friend Spotted Fur Cap.

When Bear Chief had finished his tale, Ermine Woman spoke up: "Oh, surely Sun is with you in your undertaking. He will help you kill the cowardly thief and help you recover your sacred shirt."

At this remark, Diamond R. winked at me and said in English: "If Sun is so powerful, why didn't he prevent the theft of the shirt?"

Then Old Bull spoke: "My sacred vision, how truly it warned us of danger ahead. Well, we met it. Sun was with us, so we all have survived; only Little Otter has been wounded."

"But I might as well be dead!" the latter broke in. "Unable to go on with you. Unable to use my arm for a long time, just to do nothing but sit and sit and sit! If only I could kill the one who shot me; slowly, little by little, kill him! But that is never to happen!"

"Now young man, take courage," said Diamond R., "This my woman and I will do for you: signal a fireboat to stop, put you on it, and pay your way to Many Houses. There your good sister will care for you until you are well and able to go to your tribe."

"Oh, good! Good! Oh, how helpful you two are! Now I shall not heed my pains, my slow recovery. Let us watch, let us listen for the coming of an upriver fireboat which we may be sure to halt so I can be upon my way," Little Otter almost tearfully cried.

Heavy Runner rounded up the horses and corraled them, five dragging Assiniboine lariats. With a team and doubletrees and chain, Diamond R. and I snaked the dead horses one by one down near the junction of the rivers, where the prevailing west wind would carry off the odor of their rotting bodies. We then hitched the team to a wagon, and with Ermine Woman's eager help, piled the dead Assiniboines into it, she spitting on them, pounding them with a club, and at last cutting off a dead man's right forefinger, to dry and keep in memory of our victory. Driving along the bottom to a cutbank well up from the river's edge, we dropped the bodies off it, and with a crow-bar pried off a ton or more of earth, which deeply covered them. On our way back to the post, Ermine

58

Woman happily sang a woman's song of victory, Diamond R. saying to her: "Go to it, woman, go to it!"

We slept in the big cool trade room of the post during the morning, at noon had another feast of buffalo meat, and again rested, dozing at times, out in the open. We made a package of the weapons and other articles we had taken from our enemies and asked R. Brown to keep them until we returned. This he said he was glad to do, since our presence had saved him many horses.

Late in the afternoon, Diamond R. and Ermine Woman asked us to remain with them another night, as they feared the surviving Assiniboines might be near and might make another raid. This meant that we would have to remain another day. With evident reluctance Bear Chief answered, "As you say, so must we do."

Near sunset a herd of three or four hundred buffalo came thundering down from the plain into the bottom across from us. Old Bull quietly sang one of his sacred pipe songs, the song of the buffalo bull: "When I go to water, I run." Then Heavy Runner voiced our common thought when he chanted: "Oh, what happiness it is to be in the midst of the brown ones, they our sustaining life."

The herd came crashing through the timber, spread out, and belly deep in the river drank thirstily and long; they then drew back into the bottom to rest or graze.

After another good feast that Ermine Woman prepared, we helped the horses back into the corral and gathered near it for the night, Diamond R. and Ermine Woman sitting with us for a time. Old Bull soon left us, saying that in lone quietness he would try to get a revealing vision. Bear Chief filled and lit his big black, long stem stone pipe, and as it went from one to another of our circle, Diamond R. told us that he was unhappy there at the mouth of Yellow River. He had taken charge of the trade

59

house the previous summer, expecting that the Pikuni would come there to winter and to trade with him. But they had not come. So far he had sold not even one beaver hide's worth of goods. If the Pikuni would not agree to winter here and trade with him the coming winter, he had but one course to take: load his goods on an upriver fireboat and abandon the trade house.

It was for Bear Chief to answer the complaint, and after some thought he said: "My friend, you are a generous man, really one of us. I would like to winter here and trade with you, here where buffalo and beaver are plentiful, but I am not a chief. It is for our head chiefs — White Calf, Running Crane, Little Dog, Little Plume, and Curly Bear — to say what we shall do, but when we return from our sacred quest, I will urge our chiefs that the Pikuni winter here with you." And to that we all gave hearty approval.

After some more talk, Diamond R. and Ermine Woman left us, and I took on the first watch of the night. And what a perfect night it was — warm, windless, bright with stars and a waning moon! Near and far, wolves howled, coyotes kyai yied, horned owls hooted. Close around me slept my friends, real friends, Bear Chief especially. Often, as we slept, side by side, he would put out an arm to grasp and hold my hand.

We were on the south side of the corral, my friends stretched out and sleeping close to it; I was sitting well out from them so I could see anyone approaching except from the north, from the river side. White Antelope was to relieve me at midnight. Something was wrong with me; long before midnight, I became drowsy and actually slept for a short time, awaking with a start and ashamed. I looked up at the Seven Persons, which were nowhere near their midnight position; it was, apparently, about ten o'clock. On hands and knees I crept to the corral, stood up, and looked in at the horses, most of them lying down asleep. I turned, back against the rails of the corral, and carefully scanned all the bottom land I could see, but nowhere was anything moving. I doubted that the survivors of the Assiniboine war party would return. After what seemed to me to be hours, my eyes began to water, my legs to ache. I looked up at the Seven Persons: it was, by their position, about eleven o'clock. Slowly and quietly I stole out past my sleeping friends and sat. Suddenly the horses began snorting and running around in the corral, one of them giving out an almost human shriek of agony. My friends were up and running to the corral almost as soon as I was, Bear Chief shouting: "Here again those Assiniboines. We must kill them all!" We climbed up onto the corral fence. The horses were gathered at the corral's south side, snorting and trembling, all staring at a dead horse close to the north side rails, where a huge bear was biting and tearing open the animal's flank. Almost as one man, we fired, and it fell, shuddered, and lay still. As we climbed down into the corral to look at the bear, Diamond R. and his family joined us, and also Old Bull from his lone resting place, shouting, "Why the shooting, my young ones? What has happened?"

"Another real-bear," I answered. It was a huge old male grizzly, its summer coat of hair thin and light colored. Examining the dead horse, we found that its neck was broken, probably by a blow of the bear's powerful forepaw. Ermine Woman said that she would like to have its foreclaws, so I cut them off for her. Diamond R. grumbled that he had two more carcasses to drag down to the bottom. Soon we were all again at rest, White Antelope to watch and the night passing without further disturbance.

We got up early and bathed in the river; my friends had ample time to rebraid their hair, paint themselves, and

61

put their war sacks in order before Diamond R. called us to breakfast. We were all in good spirits, joking and laughing, all except Old Bull, who sat silent and solemn-faced, not even looking at the plate of food that Ermine Woman had set before him. Concerned, Bear Chief spoke to him: "Sun's man, what troubles you? Are you sick?"

"Though long I prayed the Above Ones, they gave no revealing vision, no vision of any kind," he sadly answered. He then left us, dampening my friends' good spirits.

The meal over, Diamond R. and Owns-His-Own-Horses harnessed a team and dragged the dead bear and horse down to the junction of rivers, and they then turned out the whole band of horses to graze, except for one, which was watered and then picketed on good grass just above the corral. A little later a small herd of buffalo came from the plain down into the upper end of the bottom. Bear Chief told Heavy Runner to go and kill one of them. He soon downed one, a fat two winters' bull; we followed, butchering it and bringing back choice parts for Ermine Woman to roast for us in her big stove; there was enough to last several days.

In mid-afternoon we heard the long-drawn sighing of the engine exhaust of an up-river steamboat, and it soon came in sight sturdily making its way against the swift current of the river and at good speed. Diamond R. and I waved to it with Ermine Woman's white dishcloths, and it answered with a hoarse whistle, drawing in to shore right in front of us; several of the deck hands jumped down with a rope that they tied to a corral post. It was the I. G. Baker and Co. boat the *Red Eagle*, which Charles Conrad himself had named for our powerful sacred Thunder Bird Pipe man. Diamond R. and I both knew its genial Captain Williams. He came ashore when the gangplank was thrust out, and when we told him we wanted passage to Fort Benton for wounded Little Otter, he laughed, called to his many passengers staring at us from the upper deck to come down, and said: "I want those pilgrims up there to hear you tell of your killing of the raiders; it will do them good. I don't care if it takes all day!"

Out they came across the gangplank and stood before us, twenty-five or thirty men and women, and what a contrast they were to our group: the men in long black Prince Albert coats and silk hats, their faces bewhiskered. The women were wearing flowered bonnets and vari-colored dresses that flared widely over hoops and bustles. Bear Chief whispered to me: "Those women's behinds, so very big; is it that they are diseased?"

And did they stare at us! At Diamond R., tall and slender, smooth faced, dressed in beautifully fringed and beaded buckskin shirt and trousers, wearing two eagle feathers; at his wife, handsome in her beaded and belted buckskin gown, her long braids of hair neatly coiled around her head. But they stared most intently at my war-clothed friends, their rifles in hand, their hair neatly braided, their cheeks and chins red-painted. Clean, brave, dignified men they were. I was proud of them. Off to one side stood the shy and reserved Owns-His-Own-Horses, who was wearing a white buckskin vest, leggings, breechclout, and moccasins. His clothes were all beaded to match, except his breechclout, which was quilled. A fine specimen of young Blackfeet manhood, his arm muscles stood out like those of a wrestler, and his braids were long and sleek.

Captain Williams addressed his passengers: "Well, my pilgrims, there was some trouble here the night before last. I think you will like to hear about it." He then asked Diamond R. and me to tell the story, but after conferring,

63

we decided that Bear Chief should have that honor, I to be his interpreter. He was more than willing, and moving forward a step or two, I beside him, he began:

"A mean Cut Throat, one named Sitting Eagle, stole my war shirt. With my friends, I am on my way down-river to take it back and kill him. We arrived in the middle of the night, at the home of our good friend Brown and his wife, our relative Ermine Woman, and of her brother Owns-His-Own-Horses. We did not want to waken them, so we went close to the corral of horses. My friends slept while I sat up on watch. Came some enemies into the corral and began roping the horses. I wakened my friends, and we killed six of the enemy. The others, we don't know how many, ran off. Only one of us was wounded, Little Otter there, was shoulder shot. We found that they were our always-enemies, the Assiniboinies. We took their rifles, bows and arrows, and other belongings. Our friends will keep them for us until we return. There, that is all."

As Bear Chief ended, the men, and some of the women, clapped their hands and came forward to question Diamond R. and me. But Captain Williams shouted: "We have to go now! All aboard! All aboard!" and reluctantly the pilgrims returned to the *Red Eagle*. The Captain would not let us pay for Little Otter's passage. Little Otter looked sad, as he said, "I shall constantly pray for your success; pray that you may soon return with the sacred shirt and the scalp of Sitting Eagle." A moment later, with a short hoarse whistle, the *Red Eagle* resumed its way up river.

During our last meal with our friends, Diamond R. said to me: "I suppose you couldn't quit your war party and stop here with me and Ermine Woman and Owns-His-Own-Horses."

"You know that if I did, it would be all off with me and

64

the Pikuni," I answered, and he nodded his head in agreement.

At dusk we forded Yellow River (Judith) and were on our way again, well fed and with plenty of roast meat in our war sacks; light hearted too, all except Old Bull, who was depressed because he had been given no vision.

The Blackfeet name for Lewis and Clark's Judith River is *Otokwi tuktai*, Yellow River, as it rises in the *Otokwi istukists*, the Yellow Mountains (Judith), so named for their color.

We traveled through grove after grove of cottonwoods for the greater part of the night, now and then frightening a herd of buffalo that would crash through the brush and thunder toward the plain. As a herd fled from us, White Antelope exclaimed: "Oh, what happiness to again be in the midst of these animals, the Sun's gift for our successful living!" With that, he started singing the sacred song "When I go to water, I run," but he was not to finish it. Seizing him, shaking him, Old Bull fiercely scolded: "Stop it! Stop it! Are you crazy? You know that song can only be sung in its place in my Eagle Head Pipe ceremony."

"Oh, true! True! I was so happy I had no thought of anything but buffalo. Oh, Old Bull! What shall I do?" White Antelope wailed.

"Make a sacrifice to Sun and pray, well you know what for," Old Bull gruffly answered, and thoughtfully and silently we continued on our way.

We stopped for our day's rest in a grove just below the Dauphin Rapid, the swiftest rapid of the navigable part of the river. Steamboats ascended it a hundred yards or so at a time by means of a long rope that deckhands fastened upshore to a tree or post; the rope was then coiled in by the steam powered capstan on the foredeck. The rapid had probably been named by some early employee of the American Fur Company. However, the river men, trappers, and traders pronounced the word as though it were spelled dough fan, with the accent on the dough.

We had bathed and were eating some of our roasted buffalo meat when we heard the unmistakable sound of wood chopping in the lower part of the grove. The axe men were "woodhawks," men who cut, hauled, and piled on the river banks cordwood which they sold to the woodburning steamboats at eight to twelve dollars per cord. Theirs was a hard and dangerous life; many "woodhawks" had been killed and their horses stolen by war parties, particularly those of the Sioux tribes, but we would not trouble them. I gave my friends the whites' name for them: woodhawks. They laughed, and Owl Child remarked that it was a crazy name: hawks did not, could not, cut wood.

Old Bull broke in: "With the sound of wood chopping in my ears, it will be impossible for me to obtain a vision; come, we must go below here to get our rest."

When we had entered the grove, Bear Chief had sent Heavy Runner up to the valley slope to do the morning watch. Now I went up and signed him to come down. When he joined us, we took up our belongings and went on down the grove, soon sighting the woodhawks, three big bewhiskered men. They had felled a dead cottonwood and sawed it into four foot lengths, splitting the logs and piling them on a team-hitched wagon. As he rested and wiped sweat from his brow, one of the men saw us, stiffened, and yelled to the others: "Injuns comin' ! Grab yer rifles! Duck!"

They ran to the wagon, snatching their rifles from the ground, and dove out of sight in some brush.

"I will tell them not to fear us; that we are peaceful," I said to Bear Chief. "No! No! None down here are to know

66

who we are, where we are going. Come, we retreat," he ordered. Back we went for several hundred yards before turning down along the inner edge of the grove. When we had passed it, we came to rest in a grove a mile or more below. Heavy Runner again went up on the steep valley slope for the morning watch, and Old Bull again left us to try for a helpful vision.

Chapter 6

Wolverine the Flathead
Joins the Party

At noon, Bear Chief wakened us by shaking Owl Child
and telling him to go to the top of the slope to take the
afternoon watch. Owl Child complained of cramps, saying
he could not make the steep climb, so I said I would relieve
Heavy Runner, taking up my rifle and starting up the
narrow ridge. I found Heavy Runner at the top; springing
up and pointing, he exclaimed: "Just see them there, and
there, and there! So many of them! Oh, what happiness
just to stand and look at them!"

There were three large herds of buffalo out on the plain
to the south of us, the nearest herd not more than a mile
away and slowly coming toward us. I said that the sight of
so many buffalo did make one happy. Pointing to some
mountains thirty-five or forty miles to the southeast,
Heavy Runner told me that they were the *Koon Istukists*,
Snow Mountains (Snowy Mountains of the whites); that
the high, steep black mountain at the northeast end of the
range was *Sik Istuki*, Black Mountain, its summit a favorite lookout place of war parties. Little did I then think

that, two summers later, I was to climb to its summit and see, off to the south, north and east, the great plain and valley of the Musselshell River spotted with huge herds of buffalo.

Saying he would sit with me for a time were he not so thirsty, Heavy Runner went running down the slope. I stood for a time, made sure there was no sign of enemies out on the plain, and then sat down and scrutinized the river valley. There was no sign of life anywhere along it. How greatly privileged I was! Here I was, free from all the complexities and commitments of civilized life. Oh, what happiness was mine!

The well-scattered approaching herd of buffalo slowed and stopped, lay down to rest and chew their cuds, all except a few wise old cows standing on watch for any danger. I thought the herd numbered all of five hundred — cows, calves, and immature bulls and heifers. All during the summer, the mature bulls, in small bands, kept to themselves to be free from annoyance by the frisking calves. In August, the bulls joined the cows, and the mating season began. Unlike the bulls of domestic cattle, they did not bellow: they moaned, loud and deep-toned, the mating sound like intermittent thunder.

Though I did my best to keep awake, in late afternoon I fell asleep several times; I would awake feeling deeply ashamed, rub my eyes, and keenly look over the country for signs of danger, only to fall asleep again. But the short naps refreshed me, strengthened me. As the sun was setting, I sprinted down the long steep slope, drank at the river, and joined my friends in eating some of our roasted meat, reporting that I had seen no signs whatever of enemies. My friends were in a happy mood, derisively scolding one another or humming snatches of war songs, all save Old Bull, whose frowning silence was evidence that the Above Ones had given him no vision. Signing to us to cease talking, he began: "You young ones," but got no further, for from a nearby dense growth of willows came shrilly, in broken Blackfeet: *"Pikuni! Kimoket! Nistoa Kwotokspi tupi!"* ("Pikuni, pity me! Flathead Man!") We snatched up our rifles and crouched Bear Chief shouting to the wailer: *"Kwotokspi rupi! Puksiput!"* ("Flathead man! Come here!") Out he came from the willows and hesitantly approached us, a tall, slender solemn-faced man, wild haired, his beaded buckskin war clothes soiled and wrinkled, a war sack slung from a shoulder. Though he had two bolts of cartridges and a sheathed knife at his waist, he had no rifle. Old Bull cried out: "We know him! He is one of those Flatheads who often visit us. His name is Wolverine. He has a twin brother — yes, one named Big Crane."

We were all up, staring at the Flathead, several saying that they knew him, that he must have been in great trouble to have lost his rifle. Hoarsely crying, he came straight to Old Bull and embraced him. Old Bull spoke to him soothingly, persuaded him to sit and cease crying, and gave him a thick slice of roasted meat. With his knife, Wolverine cut a small morsel of it, tentatively putting it in his mouth; he then chewed and swallowed it, and after a moment, ravenously devoured the whole piece. We all sat down in a little circle, while Bear Chief filled, lit, and passed his big pipe, offering it to me first and signing to our guest: "You Flathead man. You named Wolverine. We are your friends. You smoke with us. We see you have lost your rifle. Now fully tell us of your trouble."

The Indians west of the Rockies did not know the sign language, except those few who had had long intercourse with the various nomadic tribes of the plains. Wolverine was one of these — expertly and rapidly, with graceful use

70

of his hands and now and then a few words of Blackfeet, he told us his sad story:

"We, my Flathead people, were camped at our sacred Dancing Lake (Lake McDonald). My brother Big Crane and I wanted to be leaders of our Flathead people. We had raided enemy tribes three times. We had returned with Crow and Cree horses, but we had taken no enemy scalps, no enemy weapons. On the next raid, we would kill some enemies as well a take enemy horses. And this time we would raid the Cut Throats (Assiniboines), worst of the Parted Hair (Sioux) tribes. If we could do that, bring home Cut Throat scalps as well as Cut Throat horses, we would surely become chiefs of our Flathead people. Three brave friends agreed to go with us — Hooting Swan, Bull Moose, and Black Bear. We climbed to the top of the Backbone (Rocky Mountains), came down the trail along your Two Sun Lodges River (Two Medicine River), then followed down your Bear River (Marias River) to your Big River (Missouri River), but nowhere along them did we find a Pikuni camp. That made us feel low-hearted; we had hoped to visit with you, smoke with you, get some of you to go with us against the Cut Throats.

"We went on down your Big River Valley, going watchfully, traveling only in the night, and in daytime seeing no signs of enemies. We saw fireboats going up and down the river. We saw here and there white men cutting wood for the fireboats. We did not let them see us. Then one morning, as Sun was rising, we came upon a great herd of buffalo and killed one, a fat young cow. Quickly we butchered it, built a fire, broiled some of the meat, eating our fill. How good it was, meat of your buffalo! How rich you are, you Pikuni, you with your great plains almost black with buffalo herds.

"We traveled on, seeing no signs of enemies, and buffalo

71

herds were everywhere — in the valley, on the great plains. At daylight one morning we killed another young cow, took some of the meat, went into the timber, built a fire on a high cutbank at the edge of the river, and broiled and ate some of the fat meat. Then Black Bear went up to the edge of the plain to watch for possible enemies, and we four slept. At mid-day, Hooting Swan took the watch, Black Bear came down, and we four slept and slept. Sun had set when Hooting Swan came down and wakened us, said that he had seen no signs of enemies. We built another little fire, were roasting some meat, when my brother said we should roast enough meat to last us through the next day. 'Too dangerous,' I said, 'our fire could be seen from the rim of the plain and from the surrounding valley.' But Hooting Swan said: 'We should do as Big Crane says. He has carefully kept watch on the plain and valley; he is sure there are no enemies near.' So as we ate, we broiled more meat. Night came. The fire died down, and my brother got up, brought more wood. As he stood dropping the sticks onto the coals, enemies in the brush to the south began shooting at us. My brother dropped straight down into the fire. Hooting Swan, at my left, sprang up, then fell against me. I seized my gun and ran for the river, the enemies yelling and shooting and running after me. I jumped from the high cutbank down into the deep water of the river, came up, began swimming toward the other shore. My clothes and gun hindered my swimming, so I had to let go the gun, but still I swam more and more slowly. Finally I could swim no longer, but as I was about to sink, my feet touched sand, and, though weak, I was able to wade to shore. I fell down upon the shore, lay there I know not how long, as though dead. Then I came alive and sat up, mourning my brother and my three friends, all of them dead I was sure. I could see across the river, see dimly the light of the fire we had built. The enemies were there, no doubt feasting and smoking, happy over the slaughter of my brother and my friends. Ha! They were singing their warrior songs, songs that I had never heard. Then at last they sang a song I did know, one we all know, the one we call the Parted Hairs' Song. It was the Cut Throat song that our long-ago ancestor Raven Chief had learned when, a young boy, he had been captured by the Cut Throats and kept their slave for some winters. They were the ones who had killed my brave good brother, my friends. They would pay for these murders: I would go home, get many of our brave Flatheads to go with me to make the Cut Throats suffer for what they had done. Though I had no gun, I had a knife: I could dig and eat roots. I got up and started up the valley. That was five nights ago. If you generous Pikuni warriors give me plenty of your buffalo meat, I will broil it and on my homeward way eat it daily."

"Wolverine, you brave Flathead man," Bear Chief praised, signing to him, "some of the Cut Throats raided our Pikuni camp. One of them, his name is Sitting Eagle, stole my war shirt. They stole some of our horses. We are now on or way to recover my war shirt and make those Cut Throats pay for what they did to us. Come now with us, and we will help you make them suffer for killing your brother and your friends."

"Pikuni chief, if I had a gun, I would go with you," Wolverine replied. "Without one I am powerless. So is it that I must go home to get another gun and some friends to go with me against the Cut Throats."

Besides his Winchester rifle, White Antelope had a .44 caliber rim fire Colt revolver in a trim holster, and a belt of cartridges for the revolver. Quickly offering them to the Flathead, he said as he signed: "This my short gun I give

73

to you. It is powerful. You will not have to go back to your people for help; you will go with us to take revenge against the Cut Throats."

With a shrill cry and smile of pleased surprise, Wolverine hugged the present, laid it on his lap and signed: "You are good. You are generous. I will go with you. When we meet the Cut Throats, I will try hard to make you not ashamed of me." Then he rose, buckled on the belt, examined the revolver, put it back in its holster, and signed to us, "Let us go on."

We traveled fast and steadily that night and at dawn we came to the mouth of Cow Creek of the whites and to Cow Island, just below it. Why some American fur company so named the stream and the island is not now known. Lewis and Clark called the stream Windsor's Creek, after a soldier member of their expedition. But the Blackfeet tribes have the most appropriate name for it: *Stahtsikyi Tuktai*, Middle Creek, for it rises between their Bear Paw and Wolf mountains (Bear Paw Mountains and the Little Rockies of the whites), thirty to forty miles north of the river. At the mouth of Cow Creek, in the low water of late summer, the up-bound steamboats were obliged to unload their cargoes. Various bull and mule trains then carried the cargoes to Fort Benton and other points, since it was difficult, if not impossible, for wheeled vehicles to reach the banks of the Missouri at other points between Cow Creek and Fort Benton.

In the vicinity of Cow Island, the Missouri at this time was about six to seven hundred feet below the level of the surrounding country and was bordered on both sides by irregular and rough formations of badlands. Opposite Cow Island, at the mouth of Cow Creek, was a large piece of bottom land. Other than at this point, access to this bottom land was by way of a trail to the north-northwest

74

(for a distance of about twelve to fifteen miles) which crossed the twisting channel of the creek more than thirty times between the flat area and the open plains to the north.

Because the river here was shallow and accessible, buffalo as well as other animals crossed with the greatest ease. As a result, the plain nearby was a favorite camping and hunting spot for the Pikuni, as well as for neighboring tribes.

I said to my friends: "It was here, in the falling leaves moon of two summers back, that the Blue People (Nez Perce Indians) crossed the river as they fled from white soldiers and headed for safety in the Red Coats' country. A few days later, just beyond those Bear Paw Mountains, they had their last fight with the soldiers and were captured by them."

Chapter 7

The Heavenly Visitor
and Sun Dance Origins

We traveled several miles beyond the Pikuni camping site and stopped in a small cottonwood grove. Old Bull suggested, "Let's stop here by this hollow tree. If I do not have a vision from the Above Ones during my sleep today, I will go inside the tree and pray, after I wake up."

Since Bear Chief wished to be sure that the watchers would miss no unnatural movements of any kind, he assigned us in pairs for the day's watch, each pair waking the next watchers. He decided not to have Old Bull or himself take a turn, since he did not wish to disturb Old Bull's chances for a vision and since he wanted to remain close by so he would be the first to hear about it. He therefore divided the daylight time into six periods, two periods for each pair of watchers. Each pair gave an honest estimate of time as set up by Bear Chief, and although the watchers were a considerable distance from one another, each one of a pair terminated a period within a few moments of the other watcher. From one pair to the next there was never any argument as to who was doing the most watching.

It indeed would have been uncanny except that these people were Sun worshippers and Heaven watchers and through the centuries had been trained in telling time this way. Also, each pair, during a watch, ate slices of meat and camas bulbs cooked previously, so that time would not pass so slowly. I could have taken along a watch, since I had a keywinder made in 1869, but I did not want to be a party to contributing a device of civilization to these simple people. I wanted to keep them prolonging their old way of life as long as possible, although I knew the nomadic life and culture of the Plains Indian was vanishing in direct proportion to the disappearance of the buffalo. Over eighty million had been slaughtered since 1850: the southern herd was gone, and only about five million of the northern herd remained. Somewhat in opposition to this philosophy, I had brought along a telescope, which, besides the gun, was the most useful and sought after addition to the Indian World.

Game was close by and could have been killed without effort, but that would have meant both the noise of a gun and a fire to roast the game, so Bear Chief decided against taking the risk of alerting possible enemies of our presence.

A path close by showed moccasin tracks not more than one or two days old. Old Bull, who was a fine reader of such tracks, declared them to be those of Assiniboines.

About dusk Old Bull awakened. He had not had a vision; therefore he went into the hollow tree and prayed: "Above Ones, please give us a sign of what is ahead. Many days have I slept and waited for a vision, but you have given me none. Have I done something to offend you? Do we have enemies near at hand? Are we about to die? What is to happen to us? Will we get back home? Have pity on us."

77

He had no more than spoken these words when his body stiffened, his face becoming tense and his eye balls rolling upwards in his head. He leaned back against the inside of the tree. Bear Chief and I were standing close to the tree when this happened. The rest, except for the watchers, were still asleep.

Before us a white shadow was forming, starting up from the ground and spinning up like a whirlwind, building higher and higher until it reached the height of Bear Chief. Then the fluorescent white cloud began taking a man's shape, the ears, nose, mouth, eyes, and the rest of the face forming first, then the body, arms, and legs. The figure took on such details as moccasins, a full head dress to the ground, necklaces, and some face coloring. As I stood there, it seemed as though I could look through the Heavenly Visitor as one would look through a light colored window pane.

The Visitor spoke in Blackfeet, "Bear Chief, I am your helper. I have been helping you all your life. I have helped you in battles, I guide you and give you good thought. My name is Gray Eagle.

"There is trouble for you ahead. How much trouble will depend on how careful you are in your movements. Do not travel this night. You all will go to the Sand Hills someday, but those who are needed here now will stay for a while; those who are needed over there to help do the work of the Above Ones will go earlier. Bear Chief, you will be rewarded," and with that the almost transparent visitor vanished into the sky in a streak of light.

As Old Bull awakened from his trance, I asked him if he remembered anything that had gone on. Said he, "I remember only that I slept. What happened?" I told him about the ghostly visitor and of his message.

Old Bull continued, "Ever since I was a young man,

there have been times over which I have had little control, when I have been seized by the Above Ones and when, as afterwards related to me by my friends, Spirit people have built up and have been seen and heard by all present. I would much rather have a vision, where I get the message direct, but when day after day has passed and I have received no message, often if I pray in an enclosure, as I did here, I am seized, and Spirit people come forth."

As the rest of the party awakened, we told them what had happened. They scolded us for not having awakened them to see the visitor from the Above Ones, for visions to them, as to most Indians, are a reality. They believe that they can commune with spirits in their sleep, that their souls, temporarily released as shadows, can travel far and meet with strange adventures, and practically all Blackfeet have secret helpers, each having obtained his secret helper by fasting and praying in some remote place, just as recorded in the case of Bear Chief.

Bear Chief took the command of the recent Heavenly Visitor seriously, and he was glad for any excuse not to travel further that night. This command from the Above Ones he intended to follow. Although we had constantly slept in the daytime on our trip and traveled at night, such daytime sleep is of an intermittent nature and is not nearly as restful as an uninterrupted period of sleep at night; therefore, we were tired and welcomed the "no travel" order.

Before it became too dark, we paired off and walked around to check the area, I walking with Bear Chief and Old Bull staying behind to meditate and pray. At the start of our walk was a tall white birch tree, which showed up well and which we used as a landmark so we could return without difficulty. Bear Chief and I hadn't walked more than 150 paces before we discovered a makeshift tepee made from cottonwood boughs, apparently just a few days before, since the leaves were still on the branches. Some war party had built it and then abandoned it.

Bear Chief remarked, "This is a good place to camp for the night. Let's tell the others." Hastily we returned to the birch tree, and before long all the party had returned, no one else having seen anything unusual. Our entire group then moved into the newly found tepee. The location of the tepee had not been selected by chance. A few feet directly to the west were three huge cottonwood trees, their trunks grown almost together at the base, which served as a windbreak. Bear Chief checked the direction of the wind, which was blowing towards the river, not back into the woods towards the plain.

"If we are careful," said he, "we can build a small smokeless fire. No one will see it, and it is doubtful that anyone can detect its odor. For an enemy to smell the fire, the smoke would have to blow far across the river, and I am sure by that time it could not be detected by man or beast."

Wolverine, who kept showing his gratitude, built the fire of alderwood. We then roasted the fresh buffalo meat that most of us had left from the day before, saving for another day the meat previously roasted by Ermine Woman. Fresh buffalo meat will keep well if it is cut into strips and packed well, as we had been careful to do.

Bear Chief suggested that we pray. Most of us prayed for from ten to fifteen minutes each. My prayer, however was short: "Great Spirit, please guide us and give us strength to serve you in the days ahead."

Old Bull, noticing the brevity of my prayer, said, "Apikuni, you have lived with us now for a long time. You do everything as we do, but you do not pray to the real god, the Sun, like we do. Why?"

"Before answering," I responded, "I will ask you a ques-
ion: Who started the Blackfeet praying to the Sun — not
ll tribes do?"

"I can answer that," broke in Old Bull.

"A long time ago there was a brave named Scarface,
because of a bad scar. Scarface loved the daughter of a
famous chief, and she told him she would marry him when
he got rid of the scar. This task was unkind and difficult,
but Scarface resolved to see what could be done. After
consulting all animals, from Wolverine to Wise Beaver,
Scarface was taken to the land where Sun and Moon lived
with their son Morning Star. All the other children of Sun
and Moon had been killed by some mysterious birds,
which Scarface attacked and killed, one after the other.
He was wounded himself, however, and returned home to
have his wounds bound up by horrified Moon. When Sun
came home and learned what had been done, he asked
Scarface to name his reward.

"When the earth visitor asked to have his scar removed,
Sun produced a mysterious black ointment, which took
away the scar. Scarface was a changed man, radiantly
handsome to look upon. Thereafter Sun took him into his
confidence and taught him all the mysteries of His power
and medicine and how the people of the earth should pray
to Him and make sacrifices. Finally, Sun gave the young
man certain medicine tokens as well as beautiful weapons
and clothes, and then Scarface parted sadly from Moon
and Morning Star, who was sorry to lose a friend. And
finally, Sun led him forth and pointed far, far away to
where they could see the earth, wide and flat. And he
showed him a broad shining road (the Milky Way) saying,
'Follow that path — it will take you straight home.'

"Scarface faithfully carried out Sun's instructions,
teaching the people how to pray to Him and make sacrifices; how to build the great lodge which they were
required to give Sun each year, and what ceremonies to
perform when doing so. Thus, through this young man the

81

people became possessors of great knowledge and learned where to turn in times of sickness, danger, and distress.*

Now Apikuni, you see why we worship Sun, the real God." "Thank you for the story. I will never forget it." All of us seemed to be in deep thought as we smoked the pipe around. The fire burned out, and we lay down and slept.

When daylight awakened me ahead of the others, I awakened everyone else, for I was apprehensive about what was in store for us that day.

* "Among the Blackfeet at festival time," James Willard Schultz. *Wide World Magazine*, April, 1900

Chapter 8

Bear Chief
Recovers His War Shirt

I noticed that Bear Chief was sniffing the air. I asked him if there was something the matter with him. His reply was "I smell buffalo." Since he was the only one to detect such an odor, I assumed that it must be his imagination. However, I do recall that on many other occasions he had the unusual ability, much like a good hunting dog, to scent various odors.

I therefore took my telescope from its case and walked out of the grove to where I could see the plain. I pulled the joints of the instrument to the right length, rested the big end on a rock pile, and held the little end to my eye, sighting down the barrel as one would his rifle. Resting the telescope on a flat rock, I pivoted it through a considerable arc. Sure enough, in the distance was a large herd of buffalo that seemed to be grazing quietly. And then I saw what I could hardly believe — a patch of white in the middle of the herd. My heart thumping, I looked again and again. Not ready for any more visions, I wanted to be absolutely certain that I was looking at the rarest of the rare — a white buffalo calf.

I had seen only one other white buffalo during the time I had been with my adopted people. My trader friend Berry said that in his lifetime he had seen but four; one ancient Piegan told me he had seen seven, the last a large cow robe purchased by his people from the Mandans for one hundred and twenty horses Like all other white hides, it too had been offered as sacrifice to the Sun god.

George Catlin, in his *Eight Years Amongst the Wildest of North American Tribes*, has this to say: "A white buffalo robe is a great curiosity even in the country of buffalo and will always command an incredible price from its extreme scarcity; and then from being the most costly article of traffic in these regions it is usually converted into a sacrifice, being offered to the Great Spirit as the most acceptable gift that can be procured.

"Among the vast herds of buffalo which graze on these boundless prairies, there is not one in a hundred thousand that is white; and when such a one is obtained, it is considered great medicine or mystery."

While I had been searching the horizon, I had not noticed that the rest of the party had come up and was standing behind me.

"What do you see, Apikuni?" they questioned in unison. When I told them, they reacted as if they had been overtaken with a fever. Last Rider and White Antelope dashed out onto the plain towards the herd, even though Bear Chief tried to stop them. They appeared to get within a hundred yards before they dropped on their bellies and began inching along, getting closer to the white one all the time.

The wind was in their favor so the buffalo did not smell them. All of the party were experienced hunters and knew well the buffalo characteristics: they do not have good eyes; they never seem to see the hunter, if he moves slowly, until he is close to them; but they do have good noses and can scent man much farther than they can see him, especially if the wind is blowing towards them. This the Blackfeet referred to as the "delicate degree of scent."

The buffalo must have smelled the hunters, for suddenly they stampeded, lunging forward in a huge wall. Last Rider and White Antelope tried to raise their guns to fire, but they had no chance, being trampled under the herd's charge. No Indians I had ever seen had hunted buffalo so carelessly, but our Pikuni friends had been lured into deadly peril by white gold.

Bear Chief screamed, "Bunch together and fire together. Take courage." Many times the width of our little group, the stampeding herd crashed toward us, their shaggy heads and brown humped backs bobbing, their pounding hoofs and the smashing of brush making a deafening and terrifying roar. The white one and its mother led the charge. Taking careful aim, I dropped the calf not far from us, and Bear Chief shot the on-rushing mother, who leaped high in the air kicking and dropped close by. The balance of our group accounted for four more, which were piled up in front of us. We had used this method many times as protection from a stampeding herd of buffalo to keep from being trampled to death, the herd dividing on each side of dead buffalo and speeding past.

As the frenzied animals hurtled past the pile of dead buffalo, we were surprised to see that the herd was being followed in wild pursuit by some crazy-brave Cut Throat warriors singing their war song and determined to die fighting.

The Cut Throats were having difficulty managing their buffalo horses, which I was certain had been stolen from Diamond R. Brown. The enemy Indians had only bows and arrows and a few muzzle loaders, as we discovered later, disadvantages offset by their greater numbers. But they could in no way stand up against the firepower of our Henry repeating rifles.

I kept on firing, this time at another target, a Cut Throat that seemed to attract me. He was riding at tremendous speed on a horse larger than the others, and I recognized it as one of R. Brown's favorites, his Appaloosa. Then I recognized the Cut Throat Sitting Eagle, who had been following the white buffalo too, some distance back. When he saw the calf go down, he did not stop, but kept on coming. He was leaning over the right side of his horse, but enough of him was showing for me to see that he was wearing Bear Chief's war shirt. As he attempted to fire at me, his gun tangled in the horse's shaggy mane. Although several of us fired, no one was able to hit him; however, for the moment he couldn't fire.

I fired, but hit only the Appaloosa, probably piercing his spine. As the horse dropped, Sitting Eagle flew off headfirst, striking the ground with a thud.

Bear Chief ran to him and quickly pulled off the sacred shirt, drawing his scalping knife to count coup. Suddenly Sitting Eagle, apparently only stunned, sprang to his feet, taking Bear Chief by surprise. The two warriors were now locked in a death struggle, each with his left hand gripped tightly around the right wrist of his foe, attempting to ward off the other's knife.

At the same instant that Sitting Eagle's knife sank deep into Bear Chief's right side, Wolverine, with his pistol, shot the Cut Throat leader through the head.

While Bear Chief and Sitting Eagle had been grappling in their death struggle, Wolverine, the only one of us without a rifle, had been waiting for a clear pistol shot at the Cut Throat. Now that the fight was over, the remaining Cut Throats having fled, Wolverine unsheathed his knife, took Sitting Eagle's scalp, and was about to sing his victory song, when he noticed that Bear Chief, bleeding profusely, had fainted. Then Old Bull, to stop the bleeding, treated Bear Chief's wound with a concoction made from yellow snowberry roots, and the Pikuni leader soon revived, surprised to find himself alive.

All was quiet now. We were stunned, as if suddenly awakened from a nightmare. A few furious moments had brought dramatic change: two of our party dead; Bear Chief severely wounded, but his sacred shirt returned; in addition to Sitting Eagle, two other Cut Throats killed, one by Owl Child and one by Heavy Runner; and dead buffalo, including a sacred white bull calf, piled before us. In an instant, sadness had replaced our victory joy.

Silently we gathered around the white calf. We dared not touch it; only a Sun priest could skin a white buffalo. Old Bull built a small fire near the sacred carcass.

Said Old Bull: "Apikuni, since you have killed him, I would like to bestow on you the honor of skinning the sacred bull; however, you are not a Sun believer, so you must not touch him at any time."

I did not reply.

He left the group and walked away some distance to a large cottonwood tree, behind which he had stored his belongings. Taking his sacred Eagle Head Pipe from its wrapping, he purified himself with smoke from slow burning sweetgrass and sang four songs. Holding the pipe to the sky, he prayed to Sun long and earnestly for full life for us all, especially mentioning me as the killer of the sacred white bull; he would give Sun some of the meat now, some later, and still later the white robe. He prayed that Sun lead the spirits of Last Rider and White Antelope safely in their journey to the Sandhills. Then he began skinning the white bull calf, while he continued to sing, this time the song of the buffalo bull, "When I go to water, I run." The rest of us, except for Bear Chief, walked out to the bodies of Last Rider and White Antelope. We did this with some reluctance, for we knew what we would find: their bodies horribly mangled, almost beyond recognition; their guns smashed, the barrels twisted and bent.

Chapter 9

Scaffold Burial
and Return to R. Brown's

We took turns carrying the bodies of our dead companions back to where we had left Bear Chief resting and Old Bull skinning the white calf. Old Bull commented, "It is sacrilege to eat the meat of a white buffalo as ordinary food. But when a sacrificial morsel is taken in prayer to nourish the soul, while facing Sun at a Sun Lodge ceremony, Sun would approve, but under certain conditions. Only at the special occasion of the ritual sacrifice of a white buffalo hide can the meat be used. This I learned from Red Eagle many years ago, when small bits of meat of a white buffalo were served at a Sun Lodge ceremony. Now we have a similar special occasion, so help me cut the meat into strips, all except Apikuni."

Although I was embarrassed to stand alone idly looking on, four others soon completed the work, and I then asked, "What shall we do with the bodies of our friends?"

"While you were gone," said Bear Chief, "I have given this much thought. Since they were on the mission to recover my war shirt and might have been the ones to kill the sacred bull, I wish to sacrifice their bodies to Sun. We have no women with us to wrap the bodies, so we must do it ourselves. We could wrap the bodies in fresh buffalo robes and then place them in trees, but bears would smell the hides and tear them apart to eat the bodies. Instead, we will build a scaffold. Back by the creek, I saw several large poles which attracted my attention because they were white, since the bark had been chewed off by beavers.

"Beavers chew down a tree at the bottom, and when it falls, they chew off the branches at the top, often leaving some heavier crotches. Find four of this type. Each two will hold one long pole between them, one on one side and one on the other, forming the platform's main support. We will pile flat rocks underneath the uprights to even the platform. We will then grease the poles with buffalo fat, adding *api-ke-ye*, a medicine made from skunk fat, which stinks and smarts. These measures should discourage predators.

"Apikuni and Wolverine, you go after the poles," added Bear Chief as he pointed in the general direction of the river. "Owl Child and Heavy Runner, you skin several buffalo, but select the fattest and smallest so they will skin easily and quickly. The sun is still high in the sky so you may be able to get the job done before nightfall."

It was hot and humid, so we removed our shirts. Wolverine and I selected poles for the platform. The uprights were to be as high as a man could reach, three poles varying only slightly in length, the remaining one shorter than any of the other three. We then selected the long poles to lay in the crotches and the shorter cross poles which would support the bodies. All were longer than necessary, to make it difficult for predators to climb over the extended ends if they did succeed in climbing the

90

SCAFFOLD BURIAL
by Glen Eagle Speaker

"Owl Child pushed the body of Last Rider into a more favorable position on the scaffold. Old Bull kept praying to his buffalo skull. Finally Heavy Runner called that he was ready."

91

greased poles. We now carried the poles back to the platform site.

While Wolverine and I constructed the platform as we had been instructed, Old Bull, continuing to pray, prepared the mutilated bodies of Last Rider and White Antelope. When he had finished, he walked some distance to the west, where he had noticed the bleached bones of several buffalo. War parties had probably taken the choice parts of meat, leaving the skeletons behind. Old Bull, who was partial to buffalo skulls, selected a large one to place on one of the upright poles, thinking the skull would give the bodies added protection. The buffalo skull was a favorite symbol of the Indians' spiritual world, having special religious significance and used in many ways and on many occasions to increase the power of prayer and to give protection against any impending danger. The use of a buffalo skull enabled a petitioner, it was thought, to get closer to the Above Ones and gave assurance that prayers would be heard and answered.

Owl Child and Heavy Runner wrapped the body of Last Rider, together with his belongings, in his own blanket and then in a buffalo robe just skinned, fur side out. After we had wound the burial package tightly with stout rawhide thongs, we hoisted it onto the platform. Owl Child pushed the body of Last Rider into a more favorable position on the scaffold. As Wolverine and I waited for the body of White Antelope to be prepared, we went to Bear Chief, who was moaning; and Old Bull kept praying to his buffalo skull. Finally Heavy Runner called that he was ready, and five of us then raised the body of White Antelope onto the platform.

Old Bull placed a number of strips of meat of the white buffalo on each of the two wrapped bodies atop the scaffold as a sacrifice to Sun. He then wrapped many thin strips of

92

meat in the white buffalo's hide, and we took turns carrying the heavy bundle back to the makeshift tepee. Included in a separate package was the unskinned skull of the white one, which Old Bull planned to mount on the Sun Dance pole should we get back in time. He would remove the lids at that time so that Sun's very own pink eyes would be glaring down at the assembled crowd.

The tepee was intact. The cottonwood trees served not only to break the continual wind coming from the setting sun, but had also divided the buffalo herd as an island does an onrushing stream. As the buffalo had missed the tepee by only a few paces on either side, branches, twigs, leaves, small vines, and trees had been shredded. Hoof prints split around the tepee, coming together again a short distance past it.

Old Bull gathered a pile of dry leaves in the tepee. On these he set his precious cargo of meat strips cut from the flesh of the white calf. Said he, "This is my plan. I will soak the sacred hide in the cool waters of Cow Creek for the night, and we may be able to get back to the Pikuni Camp before it spoils, especially if we can get horses from R. Brown. While I secure the hide in the stream with rocks, the rest of you build a fire and at each end of the fire construct a tripod between which you lay a long pole for drying and cooking the meat strips.

"We will take turns tonight in drying the meat and keeping up the fire. When one set of strips has been dried, the fire keeper will waken the next person to take a turn. We will lie over here in a row," and he pointed to one side of the tepee, "so that no one will have more than one turn. Bear Chief, who is in great pain, will not be able to help us. I have divided the meat into five piles, and by daybreak we should be finished. There is room for a fire large enough to dry all the meat."

As it was getting dark, we carried out his orders, and he placed the white hide in the stream. We had all been so busy we had paid little attention to Bear Chief, who sat silently holding his war shirt. When he returned from Cow Creek, Old Bull chewed up some willow bark and applied it to Bear Chief's wound, reducing the pain.

Before we dried any meat, we roasted some fat ribs of one of the other buffalo and ate heartily, all except Bear Chief, who had spread out his blanket and in a few moments was fast asleep. In his right hand he was clutching his precious shirt.

Old Bull took the first meat drying vigil. I was next, when he later nudged me from sleep. When I thought my quota was dry, I wakened Wolverine, and so on, until there were no raw strips left. By the time the job was complete, it had been daylight for some time.

Since we had slept only a few hours, we were still tired and hungry. While the fire was burning, we again roasted some fat buffalo meat, in large chunks so that we would not mix it with the sacred strips. What we did not eat we wrapped up for another time. Bear Chief was feeling better, especially after eating for the first time since he had been wounded.

Breaking his long silence, Bear Chief counseled, "Because of the pain, I did not sleep much. I thought much. We have been traveling only at night for fear of attack, but now we must be on the move both day and night if we are to get the sacred white hide back before it spoils. If we do not sleep until we get to R. Brown's, we can cut our travel time in half; and if we quicken our pace, the journey back might only take today and tonight.

"I will wear my war shirt. If the enemy kills all of you, I will be spared. I will take the hide back to camp, have it tanned, and place it on the Sun Lodge pole as a sacrifice to

Sun. We must hurry to get back in time for the Sun Lodge ceremonies, but we will have to get horses from R. Brown. Does anyone have anything to say?" We all nodded our approval.

We gathered our belongings, dividing up the sacred dried buffalo meat and wrapping it separately. Old Bull then went to the stream for the white hide, and we were on our way.

During the day, we saw many small herds of buffalo and antelope grazing on the plains, but there was no sign of enemies, probably because ever-increasing numbers of United States soldiers were protecting the area's hordes of newly arrived settlers. Due to his weakened condition, Bear Chief stopped occasionally, giving us a chance to rest, eat some buffalo meat roasted that morning, and even to doze. Since we were bone-weary to the point of not much caring what happened, we were able to relax more easily than if we had been alert and sharply aware of posible danger. At these stops, Old Bull watched us carefully to be sure we ate none of the sacred strips.

We traveled that day and all night, reaching the trading post of R. Brown and Ermine Woman just after daybreak. As soon as we arrived, Old Bull placed the sacred white hide in a cold stream. Ermine Woman had seen us coming, and she ran out to greet us. Seeing that Bear Chief was wearing his sacred war shirt, she asked in a trembling voice, "How did you get it back?"

Bear Chief told them the whole story, and they could hardly believe that so much had happened in such a short time. I told R. Brown how sorry I was I had killed his horse, but that it had been a matter of shooting at Sitting Eagle or risk being killed and that the Cut Throat had been traveling so fast I had missed him and hit his horse. "Apikuni," said he, "you are my friend; you are more

95

important than any horse. If you had missed the horse, I still wouldn't have him and you might not be sitting here now."

Ermine Woman put in, "You will want to bathe, for you have traveled far. I will prepare food."

We went to the river and bathed and combed our hair, my friends painted themselves, Old Bull attended Bear Chief's wound, and we returned to Ahsakwi's living room. Old Bull filled a pipe for us to smoke. The aroma of coffee and boiling meat made us hungry, and we hoped it wouldn't be long before food would be ready.

Owns-His-Own-Horses broke the silence. "While you were bathing, Ahsakwi and I decided to help you with gifts. Bear Chief, since this is your war party, you are to allot the gifts: first, my favorite horse Crow Horse (*Esa-Po-Me-Ta*), then my war suit, and finally my battle staff. This horse is too spirited for you to ride, since you are weak, so Old Bull will ride Crow Horse. Also Old Bull must wear my war suit. I have worn it in many battles and never been wounded having counted many coups while wearing it. Bear Chief, we will give you and the others gentle horses to ride; and pack horses to carry your belongings. At least two of you will be protected on the way home, Bear Chief wearing his war shirt and Old Bull wearing my suit.

"Apikuni, you will have a special gift, which will not be divided among the rest, since you killed both the White Calf and Ahsakwi's horse carrying the Cut Throat Sitting Eagle. I will give you my beautiful soft buckskin jacket, beaded and quilled, which my sister Ermine Woman has just made for me."

There was little comment. It is the way of the Indian to give thanks for gifts by later acts of reciprocation.

Chapter 10

Vision, White Hide, and Buffalo Hunting

Old Bull then passed the pipe and prayed: "We thank you, oh Sun, for these people and these gifts. Be with us on our trip home. Save us from our enemies. We will build you a lodge and give you the war shirt and the hide from the sacred white calf."

We had a great feast of broiled buffalo hump ribs, yeast bread, and dried applesauce. We lay down on soft buffalo robes, and, tired and our hunger appeased, we soon slept.

The sun was setting when we awakened. Bear Chief was excited, calling out, "I had a vision! My secret helper, who gave me the vision on Chief Mountain and commanded me to make the war shirt, gave me this second vision: Only by the power of Sun did the shirt protect you in many battles; only by the power of Sun did you get the shirt back. Since the shirt will protect you on the way home, give thanks to Sun by building a Sun Lodge and sacrificing the shirt to Sun. Leave the war shirt on the center lodge pole for the power of the Great Spirit to destroy — the sun, the wind, the rain, the snow, and the birds — until it has rotted away. Place also the sacred white calf's hide on the center lodge pole. Since it has always belonged to Sun and always will, you may remove it after the ceremony, but only if, after a time, you feel you must have another shirt. A shirt made from the hide of the sacred white calf will have even more power than the old one. The hide used for any other purpose would be a theft from Sun and would invoke Sun's displeasure. Every day place the hide on a tripod facing the sun so that the hide may retain its holy strength. Pray over it each day as you place it on the tripod. If you decide not to make another shirt, then at the time of the next Sun Dance, sacrifice it to Sun, to be destroyed by the elements.

"Since a war shirt with power from Sun strong enough to protect the owner must finally end as a gift to Sun, there is only a difference of time before the final sacrifice.

"Sun has been good to you, Bear Chief. To give thanks for the return of your shirt and for the sacred white hide, you must give your body to Sun. And give thanks also, if you expect to make a new shirt of the sacred hide before it is finally given to Sun."

"See, my friends," said Old Bull. "Sun surely is with us and protecting us. We must hurry home for the *Okan* (Sun Dance) so that you, Bear Chief, may go through the torture dance and sacrifice yourself and your precious shirt to Sun."

All were pleased, except Bear Chief. He was troubled, saying, "I am willing to sacrifice myself to Sun, but I have been wounded in the chest. I think we must hurry home to convince the chiefs to postpone the Sun Lodge ceremonies for a few days, while my wound heals. Although I can stand any pain for Sun, I will be less apt to faint when the skewers are shoved through the flesh of my chest and as I swing about the Sun Dance Pole, if I am completely healed. I will make a vow to Sun in prayer: Oh Sun, Oh

98

most powerful one above, you have helped me survive many dangers. You have given me back my shirt. You have given us a sacred white bull. If you will help me survive this trip, when we build the lodge for you, I will give you the shirt and with great pain dance for you."

Up to this point, R. Brown hadn't said much, but he appeared to be in deep thought and at last could hold back no longer. He offered a plan which indeed was a generous one. He had lived with Indians long enough to have become imbued with their spirit of giving. He now broke in, "You are all mighty lucky to have traveled in the daytime without being ambushed. Bear Chief, you are still weak from your wound, so you must travel slowly. Don't go too far in any one night and rest as much as you can on the way home. This means that you have a trip ahead of you of maybe six nights, if everything goes well, but it could be seven. And you need not be concerned that the sacred hide will spoil — while you remain here an extra day to rest, Ermine Woman will prepare it for your journey.

"This plan is of no surprise to Ermine Woman. I have talked it over with her while you were asleep.

"In the morning, Old Bull can give the white hide to Ermine Woman. She will work it over on a smooth graining pole she has for that purpose, fur side down. One end of the graining pole will be on the ground and the other end will be raised, but not so high as to cause the hide to slip to the ground. She will flesh it with a scraper, leaving the fur on to show that it is a white hide. If you ever decide to make another war shirt from this hide, you can at that time soak it up and remove the fur.

"When Ermine Woman has fleshed the hide, she will stretch it on a frame, with thongs. I will give you an extra horse and a travois so you can haul the frame. In this way,

99

the hide will be out of the sunlight on the way home, since during the hot daytime you can keep it in cool shade while you sleep.

"It may sound foolish for me to tell you how to make rawhide, but Ermine Woman must have permission from Old Bull to touch this hide, and to get this permission, you must know exactly what she is going to do with it. Sometimes I have seen only medicine men handle such a hide and give no one else permission to touch it. I know that Ermine Woman, who prays to Sun each day several times, on her knees facing His rays, will handle the hide with reverence and care. What say you, Old Bull and Bear Chief?"

Said Bear Chief, *"Oki, Oki,* you are good Ahsakwi," Old Bull adding, "Sun will bless you; Ermine Woman, a true child of Sun, may do as you have said."

Ermine Woman prepared food, and we ate as if we hadn't just stuffed ourselves a few hours before. What a fine woman she was, but not so much different from all other Indian women, devoted to their husbands and doing without complaint whatever work had to be done. Ermine Woman worked steadily from morning to night, every day and without complaint and without the slightest conception of distinguishing between women's work and men's work.

Ermine Woman reminded me of Bird Woman, of the Lewis and Clark expedition. After we finished eating, I opened one of the Journals, Volume II, that I had packed along, turning to the place where Captain Lewis described Bird Woman's easy-going temperament, so similar to that of Ermine Woman:

> July 28, 1805 . . . "the minnetares pursued, attacked them, killed four men and four women, a number of boys and made prisoners of all the females and four boys. Sah-

100

cah-gar-we-ah our Indian woman was one of the female prisoners at that time tho' I cannot discover that she shows any emotion or sorrow in recollecting this event, or of joy in being restored to her native country; if she has enough to eat and a few trinkets to wear I believe she would be perfectly content anywhere.

We smoked with our friends, but not for long, as we were tired and soon took to our blankets, but not before Wolverine had announced that he would continue with us. He was almost certain the Flatheads were going to join us for the Sun Dance. Knowing that we had another day to rest while Ermine Woman prepared the hide, we slept soundly.

In the morning we bathed in the cold stream, and Old Bull pulled the white calf hide from the water, giving it to Ermine Woman. She was nearly all day fleshing the hide and stretching it on the frame.

We relaxed while Ermine Woman was working on the sacred hide. Since I was curious about buffalo horses, I asked Owns-His-Own-Horses to tell us about his name and his business of training buffalo horses.

"When I was a small boy," he responded, "I learned to love my father's horses. I took care of his colts, feeding them tender bunches of clover, petting them, talking to them, and riding them. I combed their hides until their coats shone. They returned my affection, following me wherever I went.

"Finally I begged my father to give me some horses of my very own.

" 'Why do you want horses of your own when you can do what you want with mine?' he asked.

" 'It is not the same,' I replied. 'Could I sell one of your colts if someone offered me a beaver pelt or two?'

101

" 'My son,' said my father, 'my love for you is greater than yours for your horses, so I will give you five colts that you have been caring for. And from this day on, your name will be Owns-His-Own-Horses, which describes you better than Little Bull, although that was the name of your grandfather.' "

At my insistence, Owns-His-Own-Horses now described how he trained his favorite colt to hunt buffalo, and then went on to train and sell other horses for hunting buffalo.

"I rode my favorite on my first buffalo hunt. At first he didn't do well, but I talked to him, guided him, and soon he understood, by repeated trials, what he had to do. First using a bow, then a rifle, I trained my horse to put me in the right position for a good shot, to stay calm in the excitement of the chase, and not to panic at the sound of my rifle. I prefer to hunt with a short bow, as does my horse. I can aim a bow better than a rifle, and I can shoot five or six times with a bow for every ball from a rifle.

"When I started to hunt buffalo, I had my horse put me in position to aim for the heart, but often I hit behind the heart, making an ineffective shot. Now I aim at the shoulder, increasing my chance of striking the heart, as the animal charges forward. I like to hunt a buffalo as he is running at full speed and breathing hard; at this time his ribs are at their greatest separation, and an arrow will penetrate easily, often passing through the animal.

"After several hunts, my favorite horse guided himself with no mistakes. He went from buffalo to buffalo, and I didn't miss one. My horse seemed to enter into the hunt with enthusiasm and a restless spirit, as I did myself. As he caught the spirit of the chase, his ears became erect and his eyes strained to fix on the game before him. I noticed many other hunters. They had trouble with their

102

CAPTURING WILD HORSES
by Glen Eagle Speaker

103

horses. They did not manage well, and most of them had been hunting much longer than I. On my way home from one hunt, I had a dream: 'If I can train my horses to hunt buffalo, then I can train them for others. I will become rich in skins and other horses I receive in trade.' This dream I have fulfilled, living up to my name and happy in what I do."

At this point I interjected: "It is obvious that you are a wonder at training horses to hunt buffalo, but how do you capture a wild horse in the first place?"

"It is not difficult," said Owns-His-Own-Horses, "Ahsawki and I work closely together. We follow a wild horse on trained buffalo horses, running at full speed. While Ahsawki throws a lasso over the wild one's neck and sets the rope, I jump to the ground and grab the lasso, both of us keeping it tight until it nearly chokes the wild horse. If a horse kicks and rears, we tighten the lasso until he falls breathless. I then advance towards the horse's nose, hand over hand along the rope, leaving Ahsawki and his horse to hold the lasso tight. Now I throw a large piece of buckskin over the horse's head, but not tight enough to smother him. This blindfold nearly always tames the animal. Placing hobbles on his front feet and a noose around his under jaw, I am able to hold him down and prevent him from throwing himself on his back or injuring his legs. I then loosen the lasso, and after I pet him to restore his breath, I breathe into his nostrils, and he is soon subdued. I am now able to remove his hobbles and lead him back to camp.

"Some horses are more difficult than others. They rear and plunge in every way possible, until at last they yield, when they are exhausted and covered with sweat. Once they have been tamed, it isn't difficult, after a few runs, to teach them how to hunt buffalo; not to close in too fast; not

104

to run past the buffalo, but to follow his every movement; to stay in the right position until I am through firing."

Owns-His-Own-Horses closed by offering me a job. "Each horse I have trained seems to enjoy the action and will hunt without being guided. The reward in this work, Apikuni, is in the love of horses. Won't you stay on to work with me?"

I thanked him for his account of his heritage and his business, assuring him that I would enjoy staying on with him, but that I would have to pass up his kind offer.

The rest of the day we busied ourselves checking our packs and securing them with thongs in the smallest packages possible. We petted and hand-fed the horses which R. Brown and Owns-His-Own-Horses had given us so they would become used to us. We talked to them in Blackfeet as if they understood, and it seemed at times that they did. Towards evening, we strapped our many bundles onto our pack horses. All our horses seemed especially beautiful, since without them we would have been on foot.

Finished with her hide work, Ermine Woman prepared an early evening meal and packed up pemmican for our journey, an ample amount for the week we would be traveling. She assured us we would not have to spend time hunting. Old Bull passed the pipe, singing a song of praise and at dusk we were on our way.

Chapter 11

Two Medicine Lodges River and Ceremony Plans

I smiled to myself as we started, since the sight before me was comical. At the head of the procession was Bear Chief, wearing his war shirt. Then came Old Bull on the beautiful horse which was a gift from Owns-His-Own-Horses. Dressed in his newly acquired war suit, he appeared ready for battle. Usually an Indian dons such clothing only when he is about to go into battle, but Old Bull wanted to make use of the extra power the war suit was supposed to have. He was one of the most devout and sincere medicine men I knew.

Heavy Runner and Owl Child were next, followed by Wolverine. Following each rider's horse were two pack horses attached to each other by long thongs. The last of these pulled the travois carrying the frame on which the sacred white hide was mounted.

I brought up the rear, to keep an eye on the sacred hide. It was an easy assignment, since even in the dark the hide was visible; in fact, I could see little else. Sometimes, in the darkness, it seemed to be floating along by itself.

106

We traveled along the south side of Big River, building no fires nor hunting any game. We ate the food which Ermine Woman had prepared for us. Our every effort was to get to Two Medicine Lodges River before the start of the Sun Dance, which usually took place about the first of July, coming in a few days. We were willing to shorten our eating and sleeping activities in order to accomplish this goal.

When we slept, we would lay on one blanket, with another over us. It was warm, and we didn't need the one on top except to keep insects from bothering us. After the first night of travel, as the sky was reddening in the east, we made our camp. We purposely stopped in a meadow where there was green grass for the horses; we hobbled them, relieved them of their packs, and turned them out to graze. We lay down in a grove of alder trees. I was assigned the first watch, to guard against possible enemies. Old Bull complained about his hot buckskin shirt, which he was glad to take off. Also, in the dark, he had struck some feathers of his headdress against branches. He decided that for the rest of the trip he would carry the headdress in a parfleche bag. In a minor way, he was altering his religious beliefs to suit his convenience. During the day each watcher reported from his vantage point that he had seen no unusual movement of game anywhere. As evening approached, and after Old Bull prayed to the setting Sun, we again assembled our caravan and renewed our journey.

As morning overtook us, we were in the vicinity of Fort Benton. We skirted the town, hoping that soldiers or anyone else would not see us. We would have liked to report to Charlie Conrad (Spotted-Fur-Cap) that we had recovered the shirt, since he was the one who had told us who had stolen it; however, Bear Chief knew we could not spare the time or sleep we would lose if we stopped to see Charlie Conrad. We went on, knowing that Charlie would soon hear the whole story.

We headed for a spot on Big River to the west and north of Fort Benton, beyond the uppermost point of boat travel, where the water was shallow enough to cross. We forded the river at this point, the water reaching the bellies of some of the smaller horses. We camped at the same place the Pikuni had camped just before we started on the trip to recover the famed shirt. We found some broken shade, but we were partly in the open. Since we were so close to Fort Benton and since this was a favorite camping place of all tribes, we posted no guards.

This was our Teton River camp. No war party would be foolish enough to attack us here, with troops so close by. We slept, however, each with his hand on his rifle. I was the first to awaken. It was a little darker than usual. If someone had been on guard duty, he would have awakened us while it was still light. I sounded the alarm, "Get up all of you! Let's get going, unless you expect to stay here all night."

We hurriedly gathered our belongings, Old Bull putting his beautiful war coat into a parfleche bag — he was getting braver as we neared home.

Usually, when the tribe traveled from Two Medicine Lodges River to this camp, they traveled during daylight. Heavy Runner suggested to Bear Chief that to save time we also travel in the daytime, as well as at night. Bear Chief opposed this plan, saying, "When the whole tribe moves together, there is no fear of enemies; therefore, they travel during the day. A small party would have to trust to luck. We will still travel at night."

By now our travel and resting pattern had been well established. Each was carrying out his particular assignment with a minimum of conversation. My special job, different from that of anyone else, was to pour water on the sacred hide both morning and night to keep it from stiffening before we arrived. Also, the water washed away the dust that gathered during each night's travel.

We traveled four nights and well into the morning of the next day before we saw smoke coming from the tepees at the Two Medicine Lodges camp. The lookouts had seen us, and crowds of people were soon running out to meet us.

The children and young people got to us first, but soon we were surrounded by the whole camp, except for the old and infirm. As they saw Bear Chief wearing his shirt, and the white buffalo hide on the travois, they began shouting questions: "How did you get your shirt back, Bear Chief? Where did you get the sacred buffalo hide? Where are Last Rider and White Antelope?"

Bear Chief raised his hand for silence, speaking in a loud voice, "I will tell you nothing until all who are coming arrive. Those old people with canes and crutches are just as eager to hear the story as you are. I do not wish to repeat it over and over again."

In a few moments, Head Chief White Calf* arrived. Following him was a group of lesser chiefs: Big Nose, Little Plume, Tail-Feathers-Coming-Over-The-Hill, Generous Woman, Buffalo Horse, No Runner, Red Paint, Big Lake, and others.

Said White Calf, "Tell us only briefly what happened. The details will be part of counting coup at the Sun Dance. I won't let our people bother you before that time."

Bear Chief replied, "I will tell only the main parts now: we were in a fight with some Cut Throats at Cow Creek, and buffalo trampled and killed White Antelope and Last

* Father of Two Guns White Calf.

109

Rider. Our friend Wolverine shot the thief, Sitting Eagle, who was wearing my shirt, but not before we had recovered the shirt and Sitting Eagle had stabbed me in the chest. Apikuni killed the sacred white buffalo. To express my gratitude, I will sacrifice my body to Sun." Bear Chief then spoke to White Calf, "It is much to ask, but will you postpone the Sun Dance for a few days, until my wound has healed? Also my wives will have a chance to tan the sacred white hide."

"This we will do," said White Calf. Since the first announcement that White Antelope and Last Rider had been killed, because of wails of mourning, it was almost impossible to hear any further comments of either Bear Chief or White Calf.

The wives of White Antelope and Last Rider had begun to cry out and wail pitifully. White Antelope had three wives and Last Rider two. They would now have to cut their hair short, and each of the head wives would have to cut off her forefinger at the first joint. Their piteous sobbing and crying, and moaning and wailing brought tears to my own eyes.

One of those who was glad to see us was Little Otter, who had been wounded and had left the party. Perhaps he was lucky after all. Had he gone on the trip, he too might have been killed.

Bear Chief, with the consent of Old Bull, gave Fox Woman, his Sits-Beside-Him Woman, the task of tanning the sacred hide; his other wife Badger Woman, helped also. They removed the hide from the frame, folding it twice and placing it in a large skin of soft water. They left it there to soak until the next day. Continuing with my guard duties, I stayed beside it for the balance of the day and told Bear Chief I would sleep beside it that night. He was pleased.

110

In the morning, Fox Woman felt the hide, finding it pliable, and they again stretched it on the frame. Fox Woman placed a large quantity of the brains of a deer, with a little water in an iron pan letting the mixture simmer for a few moments. Then she mashed it together with her fingers and made a paste.

The wives, Fox Woman and Badger Woman, rubbed the paste over the entire hide on the hair side, rubbing it in with the palms of their hands. They continued rubbing until the hide was partly dry. Then, since the weather was cool at night, they left the hide until morning, while I still stood guard. In the morning, the wives emptied the water they had used previously, replacing it with clean water and adding hot water they had heated in a large kettle over the fire.

The next step was to completely submerge the hide in the water and churn it about with their hands until suds and foam appeared, as if soap had been used. They caught pockets of foam in the hide and did their best to squeeze the foam through, succeeding where the hide was thin; however, because in many places thickness prevented complete penetration, they had to turn the hide over and repeat the whole process on the other side. The process was more tedious than with buckskin and took longer, but they did not mind the extra time and effort since they knew they were working with a sacred hide of Sun; at times I could hear them praying, first one and then the other, for Sun's help. Although they had tanned buckskin many times, this was their first try at a white buffalo hide.

After again stretching the hide on the frame, they rubbed it hard with the sharp thin edge of a stick of hard wood, concentrating on the hair side. They worked fast and hard, rubbing and rubbing, until the skin was almost

111

dry. It was a pleasure to watch them work. If they were to find, after a few days, that the hide was not soft enough, they would repeat the whole process; but this was not the case — four days later, the sacred hide had become silken soft and a beautiful white. There was no doubt that the hide would meet with Sun's pleasure and that He would accept it.

The beginning of the Sun Dance now awaited the full recovery of Bear Chief. White Calf checked with him daily, and after six days, Bear Chief said, "White Calf, I am ready; you may begin."

White Calf, however, replied, "Bear Chief, you have proved yourself one of my best warriors. You may think that you are ready, but we will wait two more days. This added time, plus the time it takes for preparation for the Sun Dance, will give you the added strength you will need for the ordeal. This extra time will not be wasted, since there are many plans to talk over: meat cutting, berry picking, singing, and prayer meetings. Red Eagle, our powerful medicine man, has told me he has relinquished his authority for the Sun Dance to Old Bull, since Old Bull was the holy man who received the messages from the Above Ones which led to the shirt's recovery and to securing the sacred white hide. Red Eagle has advised all the remaining medicine men of his decision, including Scraping White and Spotted Bear. Therefore, before I give any orders, I will ask Old Bull for his approval, so I do not offend Sun.

"Fox Woman," White Calf continued, "an old woman of the Small Robes Clan, Clever Woman *(Mo-Ka-Ki)*, received the sacred *Natoas* (Sun Turnip) Medicine Roll from Root Woman *(Mab-Sa-Ki)*, last year's Chief Vow Woman. Clever Woman, expecting to be Chief Vow Woman at this year's ceremony, had also received the sacred pouch con-

112

taining the Great Lodge rattles, drum, paint, and fan of raven tail feathers. Clever Woman fell ill, and to my surprise and joy, she has chosen you to take her place. Earlier she had marked out the exact spot on which the Lodge is to stand. Later when she is able she will pass on to you these sacred articles with the required ceremonies.

"I have approved this action, Fox Woman, since you have tanned the sacred hide, since your husband has been sick from his wound, and since you are a good woman. Usually a Vow Woman[1] would have made ceremony plans and decisions weeks earlier, however, you had no way of knowing that Bear Chief, your husband, would be seriously wounded and would need Sun's help. He thinks he is well, but I believe he still needs Sun's help to be fully healed. Fox Woman, we must build the largest Lodge ever, for we have never had a greater occasion — when we will sacrifice to Sun both a white buffalo hide and a sacred war shirt. Besides, there are seventeen Vow Women,[2] more than the usual number. Badger Woman, I am glad that, this year at least, you are not a Vow Woman, but you will remember the restrictions: Vow Women must never handle meat, nor dig in the ground, or touch a bear skin, nor build a fire, nor carry out ashes from the fireplace. Sun made these rules so those performing this vow should be distinguished as being under His special protection. Anyone breaking Sun's rules will go blind. If both wives were Vow Women, then a relative or neighbor would have to perform your daily tasks. Perhaps at another time, if

[1] "So it is that when a woman's husband, son or other relative is ill or off to war and in great danger, she may if pure and virtuous publically vow to Sun that if he will make well the sick one, she will in the coming summer build a Medicine Lodge."

[2] In this particular year since there had been a great deal of sickness from which relatives of seventeen women had recovered, there were that many Vow Women. "The Medicine Lodge ceremonial rites of the four tribes differ somewhat in a number of details."

The Sun God's Children — James Willard Schultz

113

Bear Chief has taken more wives, or if he has been in danger, or if he needs to heal a wound or recover from sickness, then you may wish to become a Vow Woman."

Fox Woman was overjoyed. She could hardly imagine that she was to be Head Vow Woman. She immediately painted her face with red ochre, the sacred color Sun made from Earth, wiping the remaining paint on her garments. She fell to her knees and prayed, "Oh Sun, this is my greatest day. I feel full of joy; I will build You a Lodge greater than any other ever built; I am Your child forever, and when I go to the Sandhills, I will make great sacrifices to You; oh Sun, You are good, and I am grateful."

Fox Woman at once gathered together all the other Vow Women, and after she had unwrapped the bundle of sacred strips of white buffalo meat which we had brought from Cow Creek, the women cut the strips into small pieces about the size of a communion wafer. Cutting the buffalo meat into small pieces gave everyone a chance to eat a piece, a chance to be cleansed for Sun, the ritual satisfying spiritual, not physical hunger. The Vow Women also cut up buffalo tongues, three hundred in number — the number Sun required. In other years, usually only a hundred tongues had been used, but this was a special year; also, since the news of what was going to happen had spread, many visitors had joined us. By using three hundred tongues, the Vow Women could give a single tongue to each of the larger families, half a tongue to a family not so large, and perhaps a quarter to a family still smaller. No one would be left out, every one present receiving a piece of sacred tongue as well as a piece of the sacred white buffalo meat. Before being cut, the tongues were boiled for a few moments, and not a drop of the liquid was thrown out, being drunk as soon as it was cool.

While the tongues were being cut, some of the older

men sang, one after another, some medicine songs. There are three hundred songs for tongue cutting, one for each tongue.

While the meat cutting was in progress, Bear Chief called his shirt-recovery party together. Said he, "To fulfill our promise to give all the details of my shirt recovery and to count coup at the same time, we will rehearse the fight at Cow Creek and the killing of the white buffalo calf. I have asked Chewing Bones to take the part of the Cut Throat Sitting Eagle. I have borrowed a few tame buffalo which some of our young men have captured and corraled. One of these buffalo has a calf. We will have to pretend it is white. I have permission from White Calf to omit the trampling of Last Rider and White Antelope. White Calf thought it would serve no purpose since they have gone to the Sandhills and will be unable to count coup. Also, he believed that we should not repeat this part of our trip since the dead men's wives and relatives are sad enough without being reminded of their loss.

"Of course, there will be no killing — the bullets we will use will be blanks, and the arrows will have no points. Are there any questions?"

Since there were none, we went through the show, repeating the action several times and correcting the errors. I noted that Chewing Black Bones did not lean over to one side on his horse as Sitting Eagle had done. Bear Chief called his attention to it, but Chewing Black Bones argued, "If I lean over on my horse to keep from being shot, it will not indicate to all present the great power of the shirt. Sitting Eagle did not realize the power of the shirt, but I do. I will sit up straight." Bear Chief looked perplexed, but hesitatingly agreed.

The actual performance, according to Bear Chief, would be on the first day of Lodge activities. Chewing Black

Bones felt highly honored. As Sitting Eagle, he would get a chance to wear Bear Chief's war shirt and ride Crow Horse, the gift from Owns-His-Own-Horses. To wear the shirt was his reward for his part in the performance and would give everyone present a chance to see the shirt worn on a warrior. This show, as I called it, would increase my status in the tribe.

Old Bull asked Bear Chief, "In your vision did you receive any instructions as to when during the ceremony the shirt should be sacrificed to Sun?"

Bear Chief replied, "In my vision there was no mention of an exact time for the sacrifice. I propose to make the sacrifice the second day of the Lodge activities, since I would like to have Chewing Black Bones wear the shirt for counting coup the first day.

"Also, I would like to sacrifice the white hide at the same time. Since they came to us together as a gift from Sun, I would like to give them back to Him together. They should be given to Sun before I offer myself to Him, since the hide, the shirt, and the gift of my body are all part of the same sacrifice. I am certain my plan will not offend Sun, even though at times I think we do offend Him. But He knows we are good people trying to follow the right path."

Chapter 12

Sun Lodge
and the Weather Dancers

The place Clever Woman had chosen for the Lodge was a broad flat area about five miles west of our present camp site; at the new site there was ample room for the great camp. It was serviceberry *(Oko-Nok)** season, and each morning several hundred women gathered the berries and mashed them, extracting the juice, which would be passed around during Sun Dance ceremonies. The service berry was a rare treat, and everyone present would drink from the same jar until it was gone. Then the jar would be filled again — I have drunk such juice many times, after perhaps a thousand people before me.

The next day our camp moved to the new location, adjacent to the site of the Great Lodge. At the head of the long procession came the medicine women slowly riding their red-painted horses and accompanied by their husbands. Fox Woman and Bear Chief were in the lead.

---

* The serviceberry and buffalo tongue were considered sacred by the Plains Tribes just as roots and fish were the sacred foods of the Plateau and Coastal tribes respectively.

117

Following them came pack horses bearing the sacred tongues, white buffalo meat, and medicine sacks containing incense, paints, and costumes. After the leaders, came the long column of the main body of the procession, riding and driving. As they arrived at the site, they took up their appointed places and prepared their camp. Sorrel Horse *(O-Gi-Med-Tasi)*, the camp supervisor, now busied himself in carrying out the camp plan the chiefs had previously agreed to. His authority was unquestioned, so there was no disagreement or confusion as he directed each Blackfeet band or society, and each visiting tribe — Flathead, Snake, Kutenai, and other tribes of lesser number — to their exact positions in the great circle. In a short time, the prairie, except for the center position, where Sun's lodge was to be, was covered with beautifully decorated buffalo hide tepees, and the horses, hundreds and hundreds of them, had been turned out to graze on the neighboring hills.

Buffalo Robe *(Stomi-Gi-So-Kus-Me)* was the camp crier. Because there were several hundred tepees this year, he had enlisted the aid of several helpers, assigning them, as needed, to specific tribes or groups. He drilled his helpers in a rehearsal, so that each gave out identical information.

The criers then went about the camp, lifting the flap of each tepee without looking in, to announce the program for the following day and to give the time when the preliminary ceremonies, which would take four days, were to begin. They repeated their announcements each day.

Early each morning, the criers would call out in abbreviated form the program that had been announced the day before. Since all had already been advised of the day's program, this early call was a tactful way of waking up the "sleepyheads." Furthermore, overruns in time, into

118

each afternoon, was not a matter of concern, since they would only cut into smoking and story telling pleasures.

"Within the great tepee circle there were but three lodges: that of the Horns Society, a very large double lodge, with buffalo head paintings in black; near it, the very large, straight-wall lodge of the *Motokiks* (Gathered Women), the women's society, in proof of which were their travois set up all around the lodge wall; and last the lodge of the Vow Women. This lodge was painted a deep red, Sun's sacred color, and just back of it was placed the skull of a buffalo bull. A small freshly cut cottonwood leaned against the rear side and cottonwood branches surrounded the base of the lodge."* The exact site of the Sun Lodge in the center of the tepee camp had been marked with a circle of stones to prevent possible infringement by the above three lodges on its location. This huge lodge would be erected on the last day of the preliminaries.

In the Vow Women's lodge, the holy medicine women were gathered with their husbands. The women were wearing the garments prescribed by Sun and handed down from generation to generation: dresses and togas of elk skin; and headdresses of snake skin, raven tail feathers, and white-furred weasel. They had painted their faces red, with an outer rim of black, colors symbolizing day and night.

On the first day, the Vow Women, led by Fox Woman, passed around portions of the sacred tongues and white buffalo meat. The husbands of these women, and a number of old men, sat by to see that no undeserving woman received any sacred food, since no one of questionable reputation was allowed to have this sacred food. As each family was given its portion of tongue (from a quarter to a whole tongue), the family then sub-divided its

* *The Sun God's Children* — James Willard Schultz

119

portion among all members. At the same time, enough small pieces of white buffalo meat were distributed to the head of each family so that no member of a family would be left out. People seemed to be more eager to receive the buffalo meat than the tongue, holding one kind in each hand. Everyone then held both hands aloft and prayed to Sun, asking for long life, health, and happiness, as well as for an abundant supply of food and for protection from enemies. After being careful to break off a tiny piece of the tongue, but not of the white buffalo meat, they pushed it into the ground, and each one said, "Oh, Ground Person; oh Mother, we offer you a piece of this sacred meat. Have mercy on us."

After a prayer, each ate his portion in silence. After giving out the meat, the medicine women had repaired to a point just east of the place reserved for Sun's Lodge; there they erected a sweat-house of one hundred willows, one half of the sticks being painted black, the other half red. Rocks were heated nearby in a large fire, and when all was ready, the priestesses escorted their husbands to the sweat-house. In addition to the husbands were several old men, who as possessors of sacred medicines, were believed to be especially favored by Sun.

The framework of the medicine sweat-house was covered with robes and blankets. One by one the men crawled inside and took off their clothing, passing it out to their wives. The hot rocks were then placed in a hole dug in the center of the inner space. A pail of water was handed in, and at the same time the skull of a large buffalo bull *(Ano-To-Kun)* was placed on top of the sweat-house; half the skull's forehead was covered with spots of red paint, half with black, these spots representing shots of the enemy. All being ready inside, one of the oldest husbands of the medicine women dipped a buffalo

120

tail in the water and sprinkled the red hot rocks. Steam began to rise, and all the men, as well as the women outside, chanted the Buffalo Bull song, a solemn tune in minor chords. Then the old men prayed, "'Pity us, Oh Sun, have pity on us all and let us survive. We are building You a lodge. We pray that what we are about to do will find favor in Your sight. Give us all a long life. Give us health, give us plenty of food. Protect us from the snare of our enemy. Have pity on us. Have pity on us."

After the prayer came more songs, then more prayers, the ceremony lasting about an hour. The coverings were then raised, and the men, dripping with sweat, came out and plunged into the cool depths of a stream near by.

All this day and the succeeding three, the medicine women neither ate nor drank. They would not touch food or water until after sunset of the day when the Sun Lodge was erected.

On the second day, another sweat lodge was erected on the west side of the clear space and the same performance repeated. The next day the sweat lodge was built on the north side, and on the fourth day, one was erected on the south side.

On the last day of the preliminaries, men were busy everywhere. They were members of the Horn Society, or their delegates, whom Fox Woman, now head Vow Woman, had given the responsibility of building the Sun Lodge. They had brought from the cottonwood groves in the river valley all the wall posts, wall rails, and roof poles; they had then set up the posts, laying the wall rails on them. Usually the diameter of the structure was about forty feet, but this year, because of its special significance, the Sun Lodge would be about sixty feet in diameter. Members of the Horn Society also built a shelter just west of the Medicine Lodge site. It was here that Clever

121

Woman, who had been last year's head Vow Woman and who was still not feeling well, was able to go through the required fasting and transfer ceremonies, passing the sacred *Natoas Bundle* over to Fox Woman, who now wore the *Natoas* headdress, her elk skin dress, and on her back the sacred posthole digging sticks. Also, in the same shelter some of the Horns gathered and prayed and sang, awaiting the return of their companions who, mounted on their horses and in their war clothes, had left the camp that morning to get the center post of the Lodge. They had been accompanied by two old members of the Horn Society who had good war records. The rite of procuring the center post is the most sacred of the many Medicine Lodge ceremonies — none but the Horns took part in it.

Arriving at the edge of the cottonwood grove, the Horns went in and found a tree of the proper size and forked at the right height. This tree had grown as if it were to serve especially for the Sun Dance pole. At the top were several large, equally spaced branches which extended outwards in an arc. These branches would hold the side poles and serve as rib support for the roof. When the main pole was in place, long rawhide thongs extending from Bear Chief's chest would be attached at the top — tied loosely, these thongs would rotate without wrapping up, and nubbins at the end of the pole would keep the thongs from slipping lower.

Before the tree was felled, the old men counted coups, four each, and struck the tree at the end of each coup, finally praying that the tree would fall clear and that it would not break as it struck the ground. Younger members of the society then cut down the tree, and the group returned to the Sun Lodge structure, singing as they approached.

They then laid the center post with its butt end at the center hole, its forked end facing west; more ceremony now took place, before the pole was raised.

The people assembled in a huge circle. The women of the *Matokiks* (Gathered Women), four of them dressed to represent buffalo, filed out of their lodge and seated themselves to the northeast of the shelter of the sacred Vow Women. The Horn Society members, dressed in their best robes, came from their lodge and sat to the east of the shelter.

At this point, Old Red Eagle unwrapped various elaborately decorated medicine pipes, the most prized, by their owners, of all possessions; he then handed them into the Vow Women's shelter for prayer, later to be passed along the line of Horns and Matokiks, each taking a few whiffs. The smokers prayed to the Above Ones for long and full life.

In the Medicine Lodge, Fox Woman, the Chief Vow Woman, faced the center post, which was still on the ground. The Horns entered, and one of them, painted black, was stretched out full length on the post. Behind some robes, Old Bull performed a rite over him; he now arose, and in his place Old Bull and the other medicine men attached the sacred hide. Bear Chief's war shirt would be mounted on the pole after the Cow Creek fight reenactment. Great care was taken to secure thongs at the top of the pole, from which Bear Chief's body would dangle as he danced with his face towards Sun. Just below where the thongs were attached, the head of the white calf was placed, with its eye lids removed, exposing its pink eyes.

When the Lodge was completed, other gifts to Sun would be placed on top of the boughs forming the sides of the Sun Lodge. Near the south side of the Lodge doorway,

123

Bear Chief would place Fox Woman's favorite Sun dress, made of the softest white buckskin; she had taken two years to decorate it with beadwork and quill designs. Many present who had already seen this gift remarked how beautiful it was and how pleased Sun would be.

All the preparations had now been made for the raising of the post. From the north, south, east and west men of the tribe advanced, converging on the lodge site. They carried lodge poles tied in pairs, like long-handled tongs or pincers. They sang as they advanced, stopping for a rest here and there, until they reached the structure; with their long prongs, amid the victorious shouts of the crowd, they raised the post and securely set it in the hole dug for it.

As I stood there watching the various activities, the Chief himself, White Calf, addressed me:

"Apikuni, you have proved yourself a brave man and a good warrior. Without you we might not now have Bear Chief's shirt or the sacred white buffalo hide. We have a freshly killed buffalo, from which I want you to cut the strips that will bind the up-right and top cross poles of the Lodge together. While you are cutting the strips, others will be setting the poles in place. During the year you have had more than four coups, the number required for this work."

With a lump in my throat, I thanked him, grateful for this honor. What a wonderful people I had chosen for my own! If I had been a believer in the Indian religion, this was the time I would have prayed.

I was well able to keep up with the Horns, cutting strips into strands for binding the butts of the roof poles of the Medicine Lodge to its wall rails. While I was cutting the strips, I recounted four deeds of valour, including scalping two enemies, taking several horses, and other feats of

124

great danger, but I was especially careful not to mention the shirt recovery fight, since this would be reenacted the next day. I was applauded.

The roof and the walls of the Lodge were then covered with brush, except for a space on the eastern side left for a doorway. The Lodge boughs were now literally obliterated with hundreds of gifts, sacrifices to Sun. After all these years, the part of the ceremony which seems to glow most is my memory of a band of young people called Night Hawks, who each night rode among the lodges singing various Indian songs, some gay and high pitched, others so slow and sad that they all but bring tears as in my imagination I hear the Night Hawks' youthful voices.

Just as the day's ceremonies were thought to be at an end as the sun was setting, three men walked into the new structure. I inquired from Old Bull who they were and what were they going to do; he said that these three had been sick during the year but had recovered. They had vowed to Sun that if he would grant their recovery, they would act as the *Ai-tup-is-kat-si** at the next Sun Lodge. Since their prayers had been fulfilled, they were making preparations to fulfill their vow.

With some brush they had gathered for the purpose, they quickly made a little alcove inside the great lodge, covering the ground with layers of prickly juniper vine, on which they slept at night. During the day, it was their duty to stand at the entrance of their alcove and whistle and dance and pray, each using an ancient whistle made of the wingbone of an eagle and making a sound in imitation of an eagle's cry. As they danced, they wore a crown or headband made of sage interwoven with sweetgrass and

---

* Untranslatable. There is no English equivalent for this word, though perhaps as near a definition as may be given is "Whistles for everybody."

thorny juniper vines, for the purpose of warding off any more sickness. These men were supposed by the incantations to keep the rain from coming, and as a black cloud appeared above the horizon, they redoubled their efforts, frantically waving their hands and commanding the cloud to depart. As they had recovered after their vows to Sun, they were said to have special influence with the Above Ones, and so for the next two days many people sought out these three to pray for them.

As I recall, the Weather Dancers proved effective that year, for only one dark cloud appeared during the ceremonies, disappearing as they prayed. The rest of the period it was clear. While these Weather Dancers had been making their alcove, I noticed another activity on the northwest side of the great center pole. Red Eagle, Spotted Bear, and Scraping White were building a shelter of small branches covered with cottonwood and willow leaves — they did this with much ceremony, prayer, and smoking of Red Eagle's pipe. This ritual was the starting point of the torture ceremonies.

Just before dark, Buffalo Robe and his assistant criers announced that the preparation for the Sun Lodge ceremony had been completed.

Chapter 13

Coup Counting

Early in the morning, as the eastern sky became streaked with red, yet the brighter stars were still visible, people were chattering and moving about everywhere, long before the crier's announcements. As the stars faded with the coming of daylight, from almost every tepee rose columns of smoke from burning cottonwood, pine, and alder. This fragrance of burning wood, coupled with the aroma of broiling buffalo meat, was indeed pleasing and awakened even those who had stayed up too late. The entire camp was astir with nervous tension.

The camp criers repeated from central locations the abbreviation of detailed messages given to each tepee the night before. The Cow Creek fight, the death of Sitting Eagle, and the shooting of the white buffalo calf would precede all other events. When these three events were complete, other coup would be counted. Since we had rehearsed several times, the show went off well; in fact, it was more realistic than we had bargained for. Chewing Black Bones, acting the part of Sitting Eagle, was riding Crow Horse, who was a high-spirited steed. As Chewing Black Bones rode past the doorway of the Sun Lodge, a strong west wind blew Fox Woman's dress off the top of the lodge, and it landed across the horse's face, terrifying not only Crow Horse, but Chewing Black Bones and the spectators as well. The horse reared and bucked until he rid himself of the garment and also of Chewing Black Bones, who hit the ground about the same way Sitting Eagle had whom Chewing Black Bones was supposed to be imitating. The actor was stunned but recovered in time to complete his part. A few of the boys quickly mounted their horses and soon surrounded Crow Horse, lassoed and hobbled him, and turned him out with the other horses to graze.

I was especially glad that my part in the Sun Dance was about over. Breathing a sigh of relief, I could now relax, take another drink of serviceberry juice, and watch others.

Bear Chief, who seemed to attach little importance to the Crow Horse incident, remarked that perhaps Sun had staged the action this way so the crowd would have a more realistic sense of what the Cow Creek fight was like. By this time he was holding both the dress and his war shirt. With a long pole, he replaced Fox Woman's dress on a more secure branch, but since the placement of the shirt on the center post would be accompanied by much ceremony, he handed the shirt to Old Bull. It was a somber moment.

Old Bull signed to the crowd, since he could be seen by everyone but not heard, that all present would pray. Everyone fell to his knees and put the palms of his hands above his head towards Sun.

From the motions of his hands came a heart-rending prayer. Women wailed, and many present shed tears. The camp criers put the prayer into words for the benefit of the young, who had not yet learned sign language, and re-

128

peated it in the languages of visiting tribes:

"Oh Sun, Giver of all life. We are gathered together to praise You. Give us long life, health and happiness, and protection from our enemies. Give us many buffalo always so that we may have an abundance of food, warm clothing, and many tepees, which themselves point upwards towards the Heavens as a mute offering of praise to You and the Above Ones. Give our chiefs wisdom, so that they will not trade the lands of our fathers to white men, for gifts, either large or small, are soon gone, but the land remains. Please, oh Sun, do not let people rob us of our lands. Help us to keep our way of life. Help us each day and give us strength to keep from drinking the whiteman's firewater, which destroys our bodies and our senses, making Nothing-Men out of us.

"Oh Sun, keep the iron horse from us, for it brings people we do not want, people who kill our game and fence our lands and try to make us whitemen.

"We give thanks to You, oh Sun, for this shirt, which we give back to You. The power which You gave it has protect Bear Chief many times in battle. It is his greatest possession. In return for his shirt recovery, for the white buffalo hide, and for saving his life many times, tomorrow he will sacrifice his body to You. Give him the strength to endure the pain he must endure in this greatest of all sacrifices. Through his sacred helper, You have told him that if he needs another shirt, he is to borrow the white hide and make a second shirt, which will have more power than the first one. This is to be done only if he gives You the hide each day, so that it will retain its holy strength and only if he prays over it. If You do not approve, let us know by a sign or by giving him another dream. Our only desire, oh Sun, is to please You, with this Lodge, these gifts, and these prayers.

"Be with the wives of Last Rider and White Antelope, during their year of mourning. Comfort and keep them from all harm. And when life is done for each one of us, oh

129

Sun, give us a safe journey to the Sandhills, where we will abide with You and the Above Ones evermore."

As Bear Chief concluded the prayer, a hush of silence fell over the entire throng.

Coup counting went on for the rest of the day and was thoroughly enjoyed by all present, both young and old. While the Cow Creek fight overshadowed all other events, the recital of Chief Little Plume is worth relating, for the acting of his group was superb.

Little Plume appeared on the scene beautifully dressed in buckskin shirt and leggings ornamented with beadwork and ermine skins. Following him was his wife, leading a horse which was packed with bedding and several skinsacks containing food and some robes. He said to his wife, "I have only a few horses — only forty, counting the colts. We will go to the country of the Crows, where I will take many of their horses and kill some of their braves." Little Plume continued the story, saying they traveled at night and hid in the daytime, finally arriving in some timber next to the Crow camp. "Three Crows suddenly attacked us," he concluded, "but I killed all three!"

Little Plume and his wife now started to walk out into an open space reserved for the exhibition, she leading the horse. At the same instant, two men representing Crow Indians cautiously sneaked up with rifles cocked, stopping every few steps to look and listen.

Suddenly they perceived Little Plume, and at the same time he saw them; he cocked his rifle, commanding his wife to lie down. As she crouched to the ground, the Crows fired simultaneously. Little Plume returned the fire, one of the men falling and dropping his gun as naturally as if he had indeed been killed. The other, who had a muzzle loader, poured some powder into the barrel and was hastily getting a ball down on top of it when Little Plume dropped him with a second shot. While the Crow was struggling to regain his rifle, which had dropped when he fell, his left leg evidently broken, Little Plume ran up and shot him at close range. Just as he fired, another actor, representing a third Crow, appeared. Mounted on a powerful black horse, this Crow charged down on Little Plume's wife, jumped off the animal, grabbed hold of her, and attempted to lift her into his saddle. She screamed and struggled, and the Crow was unable to force her onto his horse. He then attempted to stab her, but was unable to do so since she held his arms tightly. Just then, Little Plume came running up and with his narrow knife stabbed the Crow, who fell to the ground with a wild yell, as Little Plume's wife fainted. Triumphant, the Pikuni hero now went through the motions of taking his enemy's scalp.

BEAR CHIEF SACRIFICES HIMSELF TO SUN
by Glen Eagle Speaker

*"Red blood, in deep contrast to the black paint, flowed freely over
the chest of Bear Chief and onto the blanket."*

Chapter 14

Sacrifice to Sun
and a New War Shirt

That evening, the camp criers again proclaimed the schedule of events for the following day. The last of the announcements, that of Bear Chief's sacrifice of his body to Sun, needed no repetition or emphasis. Everyone knew, but the announcement made it official. It was made clear that since the ceremony might take all day, it would come first. The length of time would depend on whether he would choose to drag a skull, or to swing out from the center pole attached to skewers run through either his back or his breasts, how deep the incisions were cut, how many times he would faint, and whether he would have to be cut down at the end of the day. It was announced that if the ceremony did consume all day, any remaining coups would be counted on the next day or two after the official Sun Lodge ceremonies had ended with Bear Chief's sacrifice.

That evening there were prayers and songs to Sun on behalf of Bear Chief. These seemed to give Bear Chief strength and support for the ordeal ahead, as they were indeed moving. If the sun were God, this was the time He

133

would have blessed his children for their reverence for all of Nature.

That night the glow of fires in hundreds of tepees was a sight to behold. Above the six feet of liners in each tepee the light had to penetrate only one thickness of skin, which made it appear as if each tepee were floating, an ethereal snow-capped mountain in the early dawn. The blend of beautiful voices made us all, momentarily at least, forget the awful trial we would witness on the following day; the singing of the Night Hawks became louder as they circled closer, fading as they moved away.

The soft sweet tones of these young people intermingled with the high-pitched voices of the Vow Women, with the deeper tones of other singers, and with a soft drumming, making memorable music. Years later, I wished I could have recorded this lovely ceremonial music.

In any case, this evening I felt deeply moved to be part of a culture that had existed for thousands of years, a way of life that was fast disappearing before the tide of white society. And I felt happy to have been a member of the shirt recovery party, especially when Bear Chief called us together, including Red Eagle, Spotted Bear, and Scraping White, to smoke and pray.

The singing and praying continued all night long. As day was breaking, Old Bull lifted the flap of the tepee, and we silently moved out in single file, all faces drawn and solemn, Old Bull in the lead. Under his left arm he carried a mink hide in a roll, a drum he was beating slowly. Red Eagle carried his powerful medicine pipe, with its black stone bowl and a plain ash stem. Also, he carried an earthen bowl of white clay, Spotted Bear one of black clay, and Scraping White one of yellow clay, in which had been mixed red ochre, the sacred color of Sun. I carried a blanket which I would offer to Sun.

134

As we walked along slowly, everyone was watching. Most of the camp had had a sleepless night, the camp criers had made no announcement, since none was necessary. I noticed some of the women weeping as we passed. Old Bull directed Bear Chief's attention to the painted buffalo skull on top of the sweat lodge to the east of the great Lodge. As we entered the great Lodge, we noticed at least three celebrants still asleep. They were as sound asleep on their prickly juniper vines as if they had been on beds of feathers. As they awakened, they looked sleepy, then surprised and confused, as they rubbed their eyes. Slowly they arose one by one and glared at us, each picking up his crown of sagebrush interwoven with prickly juniper vines and sweetgrass and placing it on his head.

Old Bull, facing Bear Chief, broke the silence. "You are ready?" he asked, staring at Bear Chief.

"Yes."

"You have thought fully about the great pain of this sacrifice — you feel sure you can endure it?"

"So I have vowed Sun I would do."

"You choose to drag the skull instead of swinging around the post?"

"I prefer swinging around the post."

"So it shall be," announced Old Bull. "Now I will tell you how it is to be done. Bear Chief, you will remove all your clothing except your breechclout and belt. When you give your medicine bundle to Sun, give also your clothing. Lie on your back with your head pointing north, in the shelter we have prepared for you. Red Eagle, you have the white clay. You will dob blotches of it in small streaks on each of Bear Chief's arms and legs. Underneath his eyes you will paint circles so that if they wash away, we will know he has wept. Scraping White, you have the yellow clay. You will paint the sun on his forehead, making streaks all the way around, to represent Sun's rays. Since you have the black clay, Spotted Bear, you will use it on his body. Since this clay dries quickly, wait for a few moments while we sing and pray, before turning Bear Chief over to paint his back. Apikuni, you place your blanket over in the spot to the north of the great pole, for Bear Chief to rest on while I cut his breasts. I will do this when Sun has fully appeared in the east, so that Bear Chief can have its full strength as he dances around the pole. Are there any questions?"

There were no questions, and the orders Old Bull had outlined were carried out. Then for a short while there were prayers, singing, and the passing of the sacred pipe, until the sun was totally above the horizon.

"Bear Chief," said Old Bull, "if your paint is dry, leave the shelter and stretch yourself out on Apikuni's blanket. I will cut your breasts while you are on your back; therefore, if you faint, you will not fall." Bear Chief did as he was told. Old Bull unwrapped a jagged-edged flint knife from the mink hide. A sharp steel knife secured from a trader would have done a quicker and better job, but the flint knife was one which had been used to cut the breasts of many warriors by other medicine men now gone to the Sandhills. Each warrior cut by this knife had recovered, so it was believed to be good medicine.

With his forefinger and thumb spread wide apart and held against the left breast of Bear Chief, Old Bull stretched the skin as much as he could. With his right hand, he slowly cut a slit in the skin, having to make stroke after stroke with the dull flint. The slit was about three inches long. Close to it, he cut a second slit. Red blood, in deep contrast to the black paint, flowed freely over the chest of Bear Chief and onto the blanket. The three Weather Dancers standing nearby were praying.

136

Bear Chief was in great pain, and his suffering increased as Old Bull put his fingers underneath the strip of skin, separating it from the flesh. Sweat was pouring from Bear Chief's face, and I was glad when he fainted. This did not slow the cutting, however — while Bear Chief was unconscious, Old Bull made two similar cuts in the other breast, separating a strip of skin as before. Then, from a beaded bag hanging on his belt, he brought out two service berry sticks, which were blunt at the ends. He rammed the sticks through the slits, first in one breast and then through the other. When Old Bull had finished this cruel operation, Bear Chief opened his eyes.

"Bear Chief, arise if you can," said Old Bull.

Bear Chief arose without reply. Sweat and blood were streaming down his body, obliterating the designs which had been painted on his chest, and as much as he had said he would not cry, tears were fast washing away the white circles under his eyes.

Old Bull now addressed the Weather Dancers: "May I borrow one of your crowns for Bear Chief?" All three quickly held out their crowns and whistles, each hoping his would be chosen. Old Bull picked up all three crowns and tried them, one at a time, on Bear Chief for size. He selected the one with the tightest fit, so the crown would not fall off during the dance, and pressed it down hard on Bear Chief's head. Blood began to trickle down his face, but Bear Chief did not flinch; he was biting the whistle hard. The lucky donor of the crown and whistle was pleased and was already making a replacement crown. Old Bull then took the rawhide thongs dangling from the center pole and tied them to the skewers in Bear Chief's breasts, one side first, then the other.

All this time the crowd had been gathering, but only those in front could see. The whole camp was there, except

137

the Vow Women. If it hadn't been for Sorrel Horse, the camp boss, the lodge would have been filled. He had anticipated a huge crowd and had enlisted many helpers to keep out all but the chiefs, who had seated themselves in a circle and were drumming a slow beat and mournful dirge while Bear Chief circled the center pole. The sacred Vow Women, who could hear but not see, since they remained in their lodge, were also beating in unison. From the time Sun appeared in the east until He had gone to His lodge in the west, the Vow Women appeared for only a short while, in the evening.

We had borrowed the drums of the Weather Beaters and were picking up the dirge, the leader of the beat White Calf himself. At the start of his dance, we could see the skin strips on Bear Chief's breast pulled outward several inches towards the top of the Sun Dance pole. He was leaning back, gazing up at the sacred skull. The drummers were now singing as loud as they could, to encourage Bear Chief to strengthen his heart. The chiefs watched him with firm set lips, praying that Bear Chief would keep up his courage and endure the terrible ordeal, until his skin strips should break and set him free. Women prayed with tear-filled eyes of pity. We could hear Bear Chief praying as he swung around, but alas he was not praying to Sun. He had dropped his head and was praying to his shirt, on which his eyes were now glued.

I was so surprised that I jumped up and followed him around the circle, hoping to help him in some way. But he seemed delirious. I heard him pray: "Oh shirt, you have protected me in battle many times. Sometimes you have made me invisible to my enemies. You have been my real helper. Help me now to endure this pain. Make the strips break loose, oh shirt, before I die. Oh shirt, I love you. Have pity on me."

White Calf heard enough of the prayer to know what was going on. He waved his arms to stop all drumming while he made an announcement: "Bear Chief has been taken over by the evil ones. He is praying to the shirt. Pray all of you to Sun that Sun does not bring down His wrath on us for this awful act. If Bear Chief hasn't gone mad, then he is a sinner. Pray, all of you." Everyone dropped to his knees, and with hands towards that great ball of fire, all spoke in the tongues of the many tribes present and prayed as never before; however, Bear Chief did not stop his circular dance nor his prayer to the shirt. The sun was about half way between straight up in the Heavens and the top ridge of the mountains to the west when Bear Chief's left side gave away. Hot with fever and still bleeding, he continued dancing, pulling and jerking at his right side. He had made a complete circle of blood around the pole. Not only did Camp Boss Sorrel Horse and his helpers have to restrain the crowd, but the hundreds of camp dogs as well.

Bear Chief struggled on, jerking one way and then another, as he tried to free his right side. Old Bull looked up at the sun. Its lower edge was close to the rim of the mountain where it would soon disappear. He looked up at it and prayed and then jumped on Bear Chief. The second thong gave way, and Bear Chief collapsed on the ground.

Where the cuts had been made, flesh was protruding. Old Bull knew that until this flesh had been cut away, there could be no healing. While he held the flesh, stretching it out, between the fingers and thumb of one hand, he sawed off each projecting piece with the dull knife. He then removed the crown from Bear Chief's head and placed both the flesh and crown at the base of the Sun Dance pole as an offering.

"Old Bull and Apikuni help me," said Bear Chief in a

139

whisper. "Help me to my lodge."

The throng looked on in silence, broken only by the occasional cry of a baby more interested in milk than in the Sun Dance. As the crowd dispersed, our wolf-like dogs were again let loose. Made savage by the smell of blood, they rushed howling to the circle where Bear Chief had been dancing. However Sorrel Horse and his helpers still guarded the pole, each holding a sharp knife and prepared to ward off any attack of the frenzied dogs.

When the left strip had broken away, Badger Woman, Bear Chief's wife, left for their lodge. She anticipated that soon the other side would break away, and she wanted to be ready. She built a fire and kept a bucket of water hot.

When we returned to the lodge, we laid Bear Chief on his back to rest. No one said anything. Badger Woman washed his body to remove the clay paint, constantly changing the water. Then she bathed his hideous wounds, and Old Bull administered a concoction called snowberry, made from yellow roots, as he had done after the Cow Creek fight. This was painful, but was much less so than the suffering endured during the Sun Dance. Actually, the treatment, coupled with Bear Chief's love of Sun, was soothing to his body as well as to his soul. I broke the silence, "Bear Chief, do you remember praying to your shirt?"

"I do not remember," he replied.

Then I told Bear Chief about how upset White Calf was and how the people prayed to Sun to pardon his transgression. "I will try to make up for my sin by sacrifices and prayers to Sun, but let's talk about it another time." And with those words Bear Chief again closed his eyes. He was suffering.

Because of a dread of possible punishment from Sun, for Bear Chief's worship of the shirt, we all were silent, star-

140

ing into the fire in deep thought; and there was no evening singing or drumming. Would Sun punish everyone for what Bear Chief had done? They didn't know, but they did believe that the ways of Sun and the Above Ones are strange. It was black dark when the flap of the tepee opened and Fox Woman entered. Her duties as head Vow Woman were ended, since the Sun Dance was officially over. Even though there would be some coup counting, dancing, feasting, drumming, and singing for the next day or two, she and the other Vow Women would have no further ceremonial duties. The events in the lodge would now be of an informal nature and unscheduled. We were all hungry, but since we were more tired than hungry, we went to bed early, without eating, and were soon asleep, even though Bear Chief was groaning and moaning. Once in a while he would cry out in pain and wake us, but in a moment or two we were again sleeping soundly.

I was sleeping to the right of Bear Chief. It must have been towards morning when he poked me several times to awaken me. "Can I help you, Bear Chief?" I asked.

"I have wonderful news, Apikuni," he whispered with excitement. "Sun forgives me, Sun forgives me; we can use the white hide for another war shirt," but at that moment a pain stopped him from further comment.

"Relax, Bear Chief; take your time, and when you feel better, tell me about it." While he hesitated, I pinched Old Bull, on my right, until I was sure he was awake. I wanted him to hear what Bear Chief had to say. Breathing heavily, Bear Chief took up where he had left off.

"I had another vision. Again I was walking along the timbered valley of Bear River (Marias), asking for help. I was ashamed and worried for having prayed to the shirt even though I didn't know what I had done. As I came to a water animal that became my secret helper during my fast on Chief Mountain. He was sad, saying to me, 'Bear Chief, I promised I would help you, but I did not help you enough. If I had, you would not have gone out of your head and prayed to the shirt. While you were praying yesterday, I visited Sun. On the way, I met Scar Face, who took me to Him. Scar Face, the originator of Sun Dances, had been watching this one. Sun, who was not like I thought him to be, was kind: He told me that His children often made mistakes, but since they are still His children, mistakes or not, and since He loves them, He forgives them. Also, He told me that since His children had given him so many gifts, He would lend the white hide so that another shirt could be made from it, but only if the shirt were offered to Him each day with prayers.

"Again the same old man appeared wearing another war shirt, the background of which was yellow. It was essentially the same pattern as the one sacrificed to Sun, with some changes. The shoulders on the front of the shirt had been painted red, except for four blue tepees on each side. The tepees pointed upwards toward the seam of the shirt.

"Also in red were pyramid designs on a long triangular neck-piece extending half way down the front of the shirt. At the bottom of each sleeve were two triangles of cut leather, and on the front and back of the shirt hung two weasel skins with red feathers and cloth. This shirt was also pierced with many small round holes in the areas covered by red paint.

"Said the water animal, 'The old man's appearance gives assurance of Sun's approval to make another war shirt.' Having said that, the shadowy old man and my secret helper vanished. This vision startled me so much that I awakened quickly and poked you."

142

Old Bull was not long in getting to his feet. He hurried to White Calf's lodge to report the vision to the chief, who was sound asleep, as were the others inside his lodge. Old Bull announced himself several times before waking those inside and being invited in. They were all startled. "What brings you here, Old Bull, so early in the morning?" said White Calf.

Old Bull related the story to an excited White Calf, who said, "Old Bull, go tell Buffalo Robe so that he and his helpers can make the announcement to the entire camp."

Old Bull did as he was told, and early in the morning the camp criers announced the good news:

"Sun has forgiven Bear Chief; Sun has forgiven Bear Chief. He gives permission to use the white hide to make another war shirt," echoed throughout the camp. News travels fast in an Indian camp. The story that Bear Chief and I related to a few, was quickly picked up by others, and soon the whole camp knew it. Because of the good news, more feasting and praying took place than had been anticipated. Many who had planned to leave that day stayed on. Only a few broke camp, and many participated in additional coup counting.

There had never been a Sun Dance like this one. On the following morning a large number of tepees were taken down and the trappings and furnishings inside were packed and placed on travois. I watched some groups as they moved away, obviously in no hurry. I could see them look up at the shirt and at the white hide on the Sun Dance pole. They seemed to be leaving with some regret.

On the next day more tepees would leave, and each day following would add a few more. Because of Bear Chief's wounds, we stayed on for several days with a few others who hated to think that the ceremony was over. This particular Sun Dance had been a memorable one, perhaps

143

BEAR CHIEF'S WAR SHIRT
by Glen Eagle Speaker

more so that any other in Blackfeet history. It had been a deep religious experience symbolizing the closeness of a simple people and their intense love for each other and for their Sun God and their Above Ones.

It was a month later when Bear Chief, his wives, and a number of other chiefs and friends returned, made camp, and with much ceremony took the white hide from the Sun Lodge pole. He had decided that he wanted another shirt. I was there, too, to witness the rare removal of a sacrifice from a Sun Lodge. I had heard of sacrifices being stolen after Sun Lodge ceremonies, probably by thieves with no faith in the Sun God, but before this time I had never seen the intentional removal of a Sun Lodge sacrifice.

When the ceremonies were over, I walked around to several other lodges of other years. They seemed intact, none of the sacrifices having been removed. They were weather-beaten, and birds of one kind or another had pecked at them, but human hands had not touched them.

Fox Woman carefully spread the sacred white hide, hair side up, and covered it with a paste made of ashes and water. She let the hide soak in this mixture for about three days, when the hair was scraped off easily. Then she took the hide and sewed it in the form of a conical bag, which she suspended on a tripod over a smudge fire built of white cedar sticks. In about ten minutes the hide was as yellow as Bear Chief's vision had pictured it.

Since Bear Chief wished to have the finest shirt possible, he selected a number of experienced shirt makers, requesting their help. They were happy to work on the shirt, since it was an honor to touch and to work on the sacred hide. Bear Chief's brother-in-law Big Plume offered his services. He had been converted to Christianity by Father DeSmet and had a suggestion to make. "If in a

145

number of places the pattern of many small holes were cut in the form of crosses, the shirt would have more power than a shirt with the sun on the front and the blue morning star on the back. Now, if you do that, I don't know what you will call it, but I will call it the Lord's Shirt." Bear Chief consented, apparently pleased.

Fox Woman added beautiful decorations to the shirt, and Bear Chief wore it in a number of battles, but the day of Indian fighting Indian would soon be over. Such fighting had already been outlawed by the United States Government. A new way of life with a new culture was fast obliterating the old, bringing many changes. The implements and tools of Indian wars would soon be found only in museums. Bear Chief would soon not need his war shirt.

As Bear Chief's need for protection from his war shirt became less, so did his regard for the shirt diminish, and eventually he was willing to relinquish it. After passing through several hands, the shirt came to the collection of Indian Americana at the Denver Art Museum. No myth, this famed Indian relic is now on display for visitors to marvel at for its color, design, and decoration.